PIG HEARTED

PIG HEARTED

ALEX PERRY

LITTLE, BROWN AND COMPANY

New York   Boston

Cover art copyright © 2021 by Ramona Kaulitzki. Cover design by Jenny Kimura. Cover copyright © 2021 by Hachette Book Group, Inc.

Little, Brown and Company
Hachette Book Group
1290 Avenue of the Americas, New York, NY 10104
Visit us at LBYR.com

First Edition: October 2021

Little, Brown and Company is a division of Hachette Book Group, Inc. The Little, Brown name and logo are trademarks of Hachette Book Group, Inc.

The publisher is not responsible for websites (or their content) that are not owned by the publisher.

Smiling emoji © Cosmic_Design/Shutterstock.com

Library of Congress Cataloging-in-Publication Data
Names: Perry, Alex, 1990- author.
Title: Pighearted / by Alex Perry.
Description: First edition. | New York : Little, Brown and Company, 2021. | Includes bibliographical references. | Audience: Ages 8-12. | Summary: In alternate chapters, twelve-year-old Jeremiah, who has a fatal heart condition, and J6, the pig growing the heart that could save his life, give their own perspectives on being a transplant donor and donee. Includes facts about the research project on which the story is based.
Identifiers: LCCN 2020054851 | ISBN 9780316538770 (hardcover) | ISBN 9780316538800 (ebook) | ISBN 9780316538817 (ebook other)
Subjects: CYAC: Human-animal relationships—Fiction. | Heart—Abnormalities—Fiction. | Transplantation of organs, tissues, etc.—Fiction. | Pigs—Fiction. | Brothers and sisters—Fiction. | Genetic engineering—Fiction.
Classification: LCC PZ7.1.P447663 Pig 2021 | DDC [Fic]—dc23
LC record available at https://lccn.loc.gov/2020054851

ISBNs: 978-0-316-53877-0 (hardcover), 978-0-316-53880-0 (ebook)

Printed in the United States of America

LSC-C

Printing 1, 2021

To Dad

CHAPTER ONE

BOY

My heart stopped before the game started.

The team was chanting in the huddle, and Paloma's hand touched mine. I felt a flutter in my chest. I thought it meant one of the butterflies in my stomach got out. It didn't.

My team shouted, threw their hands in the air, and ran to their positions. I stood still and jabbed at the new scar under my collarbone. I tried to push the flat box under my skin deeper inside my chest. That little box was my ICD, which had wires that work like defibrillator paddles, and they could either give a huge jolt to my heart or a tingling shock I could barely feel.

Paloma looked at me like I was about to drop dead.

She was the fastest kid in sixth grade because her legs were long, but she liked playing sweeper so she could keep an eye on the game.

"Jeremiah, are you okay? Are you sick?" she asked.

I was supposed to be on the other side of the field beside Adnan. I shook my head.

She caught Coach's eye and waved to him.

"I'm fine," I insisted.

"You should rest if you need to."

Coach blew his whistle and called a time-out.

A girl from the other team with curly pink hair yelled at me from across the field.

"Little boy! Little boy!"

My name is Jeremiah, not "little boy," and there are two girls in my grade who are at least an inch shorter. Pink Hair clapped at me with each word. "There. Are. No. Time-outs. In. Soccer."

I felt small. Well, smaller. I wanted to be in Dynamo Stadium, with twenty thousand fans cheering while I scored like Andrés Rossi. Instead, I stood awkwardly on a patchy field in Pelican Bayou Park, and everyone in the stands looked up from their phones to gape at me like goldfish. Coach ran over and led me away from the other players.

"You all right?"

There's never actually been anything wrong. I'd never even had a heart attack and I was almost twelve. I was fine. I deserved to run. I could get a dog and walk him for miles, but Dr. Willis said I needed a transplant as soon as my new heart was ready. Until then, I was property of the ICD. Adnan says it's like the arc reactor in Iron Man's chest that keeps him alive. He's wrong. It's just a generator under my skin that's smaller than Coach's stopwatch. It doesn't let me fly, but it's the only thing that could restart my heart. I wasn't allowed to play soccer until I got it. Even then, I had to beg Dr. Willis and my parents for months before they let me out here. I wouldn't let the least interesting thing about me ruin my life.

"Thanks, but I'm fine. Just a little nervous."

Coach smiled and said, "Then get to your position." He patted me on the shoulder and jogged off the field.

I walked to my spot and told my heart to calm down. It felt like I'd been running. Adnan was watching me carefully. I gave him a thumbs-up.

"You got this, Iron Man," he said.

Then Coach blew the whistle, and the ball flew through the air. I took off after it.

A raindrop rolled down my face. I looked up, but there wasn't a cloud in sight. It was just sweat. It was August in Houston, but according to Dad's weather app it wasn't supposed to get brain-meltingly hot until after lunch. Yet for some reason, I was already gross. Paloma probably could smell me from across the field. As sweeper, she always watched the ball, but this time I hoped she was watching me. She caught me staring and pointed to my right.

There wasn't time to be embarrassed. I turned my head, and the pink-haired girl had the ball. I fought to close the distance and show her what a "little boy" could do. My steps thundered louder than the deep bass of my heartbeat, and nothing could stop me. Freedom.

Pink Hair inched closer to the penalty area. Near me. Time to take the ball and force her off the field. I could already taste the off-brand Gatorade Adnan would pour over my head after I won the game.

Pink Hair's shoulders turned toward the line. My heart vibrated. Excitement. Maybe. All the warmth in my body drained away.

Then it happened. Her foot slipped in the dew, and the ball rolled right in front of me. I took control of it. This was my chance, but something didn't feel right.

Pink Hair caught up to me.

"I'm open!" Adnan yelled, but I needed to try for the goal. Pink Hair got closer. I dribbled faster.

"Over here, Jeremiah! Pass the ball!" Adnan yelled. Someone was coming up behind me. I kicked the ball again and pushed myself harder. The goal was so close.

Goose bumps popped onto my sweaty arm. Someone's cheering for me.

"Jeremiah! Jeremiah!"

The air thinned as if I had just sprinted up the stairs of a skyscraper.

My legs stopped working and I almost fell. I recovered, but a foot darted in front of me and the ball was gone. My heart sank into my stomach. Breathe in. Breathe in.

"Jeremiah!"

My heart quieted. Heavy. Bricks on my chest. Can't get them off. Bricks in my chest. Can't take them out. Pulling me down. A mountain of bricks on top of me. Crushing me. I tried to call for Dad, but I might as well have been buried alive.

"Jeremiah!" Dad yelled, running to me. Dad got fuzzy.

A jolt ripped through my chest. It felt like someone shot a ball out of a cannon that hit me in the back. I fell forward. The world twisted around itself, and it got too dark to tell if it stopped. Too dark to see the ball. Or Dad.

With dew on my cheek, dirt in my mouth, and the smell of cut grass in my nose, Pink Hair shouted through the blackness, "Give him a red card. He's obviously faking it."

CHAPTER TWO

PIG

I'm Jeremiah Six and I'm a pig. Kind of. Actually, Dr. Willis says I'm a chimera, which in my case means I'm a pig, but I have a human heart. Don't hold that against me. I consider myself pighearted.

I have always lived in room 23 and slept in a bed as soft as a dropped burrito. Butlers scooped pellets into my bowl, and I made bigger pellets in my corner bathroom. Best of all, I've lived next to my brothers ever since I could remember. We had our own separate plastic enclosures, but we could see and hear each other.

Dr. Willis had named us all Jeremiah. We looked the same because we were all pigs and chimeras. Jeremiah One was a hot mess. The doctors called him deranged.

Jeremiah Two was feisty but stuck up. Jeremiah Three was adventurous. Jeremiah Four was restless. Jeremiah Five was all heart. He'd push his nose to the plastic wall. It meant *I love you.*

Then there was me. I was the smart one. And the funny one. And the brave one. And the accurate-at-describing one. I also had a special power. If I made my thoughts still and quiet, I could hear my own pigheartedness deep inside. I'd tell myself the one most important word in the world. Of course, I've had to keep it to myself because pigs can't talk.

I understood doctors, but they only understood me when I bit them. I tried to tell them I didn't like stabbers or pinchers, but doctors aren't smart. Biting is the universal language. Jeremiah One was fluent in it.

When we were little, we were cute. When we got older, we were revolting. *Revolting* means "rebelling." Jeremiah One started it. He would scream at the doctors even if they didn't bring stabbers. He bit the butlers so hard blood came out. Then Jeremiah Two started doing the same thing. Then Three. All the way down the line. After everyone was revolting, the doctors took Jeremiah One away.

A few days later, Dr. Willis gave us our own TV! She said that she hoped it would "calm us down."

A TV is a big black box. Dr. Willis called it an old piece of junk. I called it a bribe. It worked. It was a great gift, but the greatest gift was the words and pictures it gave me. Everything made sense after I started watching. For example, I didn't know that I was uneducated. *Uneducated* means that you don't know anything about anything because the school bus doesn't stop at room 23. I guess the TV was supposed to teach us everything we needed to know.

The TV was the kind of substitute teacher that also made threats: "All it takes is a pig and ten bucks and you can have a charbroiled pulled-pork sandwich on an artisan bun with a large order of fries and a drink included." Then, the restaurant clown on TV would smile and stare at me while taking a huge bite of the sandwich. That meant I needed to hide under my cushion. I didn't want to be charbroiled.

After Jeremiah One left, it got quiet. I became the new bad boy. That's why the doctors decided to give me an ear tattoo. They took me to the X-ray room and stuck my legs in metal leg cuffs.

Give me a skull with a snake coming out of its eye and a dagger sticking out of the top, I said. But all they heard was "Oink." The tattoo was on my ear, so I couldn't watch them or admire it when they were done.

I changed my mind about the tattoo when I learned it involved sticking my ear in an ear chomper. I informed the doctors that I did not want a tattoo anymore by biting them. But they just put the muzzle on me. I hated it. Muzzles were for animals. Muzzles weren't for me.

I still had four brothers left. They all got matching tats. A few weeks after our tattoos, two of my brothers shuffled out of room 23 on blue leashes. They weren't like Jeremiah One. They didn't hurt anyone. Jeremiah Three and Four were the best little porkers I'd ever seen. Right before they left, they were calmer and quieter than ever. They threw up a little and laid still most of the time, but they still got taken.

I'd never put up with something like that. If it were me, I'd fight. Later, Jeremiah Two left. He had purple ears and was asleep when he got wrapped in blue blankets. He rode out on the Magic Table. None of them ever came back.

Then Jeremiah Five started throwing up. I tried to warn him about the doctors, but Dr. Willis said "he wasn't the crispiest bacon in the pan." He was all heart and no brain.

Then the next day, he was too tired to stand. He slept with his eyes open. Dr. Willis came in to feed us, but she noticed Jeremiah Five and ran over to him.

Watch out. Bite her! I screamed through the plastic wall.

Dr. Willis put a blue leash around my brother's neck. He didn't move. I noticed my door. Dr. Willis left it cracked open.

I didn't know what to do. I closed my eyes, concentrated, and my pigheartedness whispered the most important word in the world: *brother*.

I could try to run out and knock her down. I could save him. Instead, I hid under my cushion.

A butler helped slide Jeremiah Five onto the Magic Table. Dr. Willis pulled on the table until it grew tall. She folded a blue blanket over him. His eyes were still open, but he wouldn't look at me. I peeked my head out a little farther. I needed to see him one last time, but I couldn't run to him. If I tried anything, I might get taken away, too.

Don't leave! You're too handsome to go.

He looked like me until his ears turned purple.

Dr. Willis wheeled him out the door.

I'll miss you, and I love you, Jeremiah Five, I said.

I didn't save my brother. I oinked from under my cushion. It didn't matter how much I wanted him back. Nothing a pig wanted mattered. The problem with being pighearted is that your heart can tell you exactly what to do, but you aren't allowed to listen to it.

Afterward, it was just me, my butlers, and the

doctors. Doctors and butlers are the two types of people. People are like pigs, except people get to decide what they do. Also, most of them are as ugly on the outside as they are on the inside. That's why they have to wear clothes all the time. Doctors are like butlers. The difference is doctors only touch poop for medical purposes. Butlers collect it in treasure buckets and kept it forever. Sometimes the butlers pet me or talk to me. One time they even dropped a burrito on my head. That was the happiest day of my life. Butlers are almost as nice as pigs. They didn't take my brothers away.

When the doctors checked on me, I'd give them a piece of my mind. I was revolting again.

What's wrong with you? What have you done to him? I trusted you, Dr. Willis. I'd give you zero out of five stars. I would not recommend living in room 23! How would you like it if I took your brothers? What if I took Dr. Horton or Dr. Fryer?

All that came out was "Oink!" That's why I was embarrassed about having a human heart. Humans are people, and people's hearts don't work right. If they did, how could they leave me all alone? From then on, I bit any doctor who stuck a hand into my room. Vengeance tasted better than burritos.

One day, Dr. Willis and Dr. Horton rushed in.

What's wrong with you guys? I asked, but all they heard was "Oink."

They looked as upset as they did when they found Jeremiah Five sleeping with his eyes open. Dr. Willis seemed like she was going to cry.

Dr. Horton pulled up a screen, and they both stared at something that might be a close-up of a pepperoni pizza. She said it was my X-ray. That's actually my best angle because real beauty is on the inside. Dr. Willis zoomed in and looked at it very carefully.

"I think it'll work," she finally said. "The septum between the ventricles is fully formed. No trace of malformation, or under- or overdevelopment. All he needs is a few more months. Jeremiah has a real chance."

She looked relieved. Staring at my scans had that effect on people. It's not often that you get to look at something as perfect as me. Dr. Willis turned to me and bent over to scratch my head.

"Little guy, I think we've done it. I think we can save his life."

CHAPTER THREE

BOY

Adnan sat with me in the hospital room. It was quiet until something behind me started beeping. I jumped. I tried to turn to see the screen, but tubes and wires tied me down.

"You should have seen the look on her face when the ambulance came," Adnan said. "I know her. She was still whining about you needing a red card. Her name's Monica. It was funny to see her face when she called you a faker and then the EMTs flew across the field like the angel Jibreel. But you missed it because you weren't paying attention."

Either Mom or Dad had been with me the whole time I was in the hospital, but today they had to go see

Dr. Willis at Gen-e-heart next door. We were waiting for the operating room to be ready so the doctors could put a pump in my heart. It was important, but I didn't want them to take me before my family got back. At least Adnan kept me company. Paloma was probably busy. She'd just make me nervous anyway. She worries too much.

Three nurses and two people in lab coats fluttered into the room. Adnan shrank into the corner like an owl. He kept turning his head and his eyes were huge. No one made him leave.

The doctors and nurses poked me, rolled me, and looked at the screens. They spoke quickly but not to me.

"What's wrong? What's going on?" I asked.

"Nothing, we might need to put you under in a little while, but there's nothing wrong."

Is it illegal for a doctor to lie?

"Just wait here, kiddo."

The doctor forgot my name. They left. For a horrible second, I thought I was alone. Then Adnan appeared beside me. He towered over the bed. If we were both standing, I'd still look tiny. Every time he walked through a door; he'd slap the top of the doorway. Some times he barely had to jump.

We've been friends since I moved to Houston at the

end of fourth grade, but I was never able to catch up to his height. Dr. Willis said I was growing fine, but I googled it and I think my heart was slowing me down. Seeing Adnan reminded me that I was different. But listening to him joke around made me forget again.

"You'd do anything to get out of a game."

"What?" I checked the machine behind my head again.

"Are you trying to get out of talking to me by running off with some doctors? Well, too bad, because I'm going to be annoying you until you're back at school."

I looked at my blanket.

"Man, I've heard of faking an injury, but you got an ambulance and a hospital room and no one even touched you," Adnan said, watching my face. He didn't know it really was my fault.

"The doctors think something's wrong. They're not telling me everything," I said.

Adnan pretended not to hear me. He stared out the window that faced the hospital courtyard. "Did you know you're a little bit of a ball hog? I know you have other things to worry about, but have you ever heard of actually passing the ball? I was open the whole time. I thought this would be a good time to bring it up. Since you can't go anywhere."

I tried to hit him. I missed and laughed. I took a minute to catch my breath. Adnan waited.

"You know, Paloma cried when the ambulance came. She was so scared. But don't worry, as soon as she realized that we'd get to replace you on the team, she got over it." Adnan winked, then stared at me. "What really happened? Was it a heart attack? I noticed that you didn't seem to be doing good. I wanted you to slow down, that's why I kept yelling at you to pass. I thought the thing in your chest was supposed to..." He mimed defibrillator paddles on himself. Then he mimed getting shocked and fell down on the floor with his tongue out.

I turned away from him.

He didn't know that I had realized I was in trouble.

He hopped back up and held my hand like my dad would. Like I was a little boy. I'm not. I snatched my hand away. Adnan either roasts his friends without mercy, or hugs and holds their hands like Mom does with my little sister, Justus.

"Are you feeling okay? What caused it? I mean, I know there's always been this problem, but why now?"

I felt like I'd been running instead of lying in a hospital bed talking. I caught my breath. "I need a new heart. I was born with thick heart walls. They don't pump good.

When I ran, my heart"—I took a breath in—"started working too hard. They can't fix it."

A nurse appeared, ran an icy sensor over my chest, and made a worried face. He left without saying anything.

"If Jazmine had a heart, she could give you hers. She's your big sister, so it would work."

I had to wait until I was around twelve to get a new heart. I started getting ready after I turned eleven. Dr. Willis said it would be a few months before I could get the surgery. She gets people hearts. Mom and Dad say she's saved other kids like me.

"Jazmine wants to be a doctor, so I'm surprised she isn't here. She could experiment on you for free. Wait, isn't it yours and Jazmine's birthday soon?"

"Yeah."

Adnan jumped out of his chair. "Did you get her a present yet? She'll be mad. She won't care if you were in the hospital. She wouldn't care if you were dead. She'd still kill you. How about I save your life and get her a card? Your sister's birthday is the same day yours is. You should remember it."

"Yeah." I didn't want Adnan to go, but he jogged down the hall anyway.

A nurse and two orderlies burst in. They were going to

take me, and Adnan would come back to an empty room. I didn't know what would happen. Maybe I wouldn't come back. Maybe I'd never see Adnan and my parents again. Maybe I would die, and they'd have to go see me in a drawer in the basement. The nurse pushed some buttons on my bed and left. I stared at the door and tried to make Adnan reappear using psychic powers I didn't have.

But it worked this time. He returned from the gift shop with a card showing an old lady smiling without teeth. I signed it, "Happy birth day too you. From J to J." Adnan set it on my bag.

"Perfect! She'll definitely know you wrote it."

What did he mean by that?

"Now I'll solve your other problems. I'll find your evil twin, fight him, and rip his heart out. Then I'll stick it in you. Unless you're the evil twin and he's the good twin, then we'll just ditch you."

I smiled.

"There's already a math test this week for the rest of us. Not you, though. Lucky."

I turned my face away and pretended to look out the window. I nodded.

"So, when do you get to come back?"

My cheeks warmed up, and I tried to stop myself from crying.

Adnan turned his back and walked across the room.

"Do you think it'd be bad if I unplugged this?" Adnan stood next to a steel beeping machine with a large, flat monitor. It probably kept me alive. "I like having you around, but I'm also curious."

I laughed so hard I didn't notice the nurse and orderlies sweep in and surround me. I'd be fine. If I was in danger, then how could Adnan keep messing around? I could still hear him shouting jokes at me as they rolled me down the hall.

PIG

After Dr. Willis made my brothers into pigs in a blanket, I watched a lot more TV. It held a whole universe inside. It showed me things I didn't even know to wish for.

Once, I saw a movie about a place called an *orphanage*. An orphanage is a kid zoo where people watch children sing and dance. Sometimes people will go to the kid zoo and pick out the cutest singer and dancer and take them home. They leave the other kids there until they get cuter. The people who take you home become your parents.

Parents were the tallest members of the family. But there were other family members, too. They're called brothers. Sometimes brothers are boys, and sometimes they are girls.

If you're a part of a family, then you have it made. You get a whole giant room with a bed and no one puts you in a sandwich. No one wraps you in blankets and takes you away. The TV showed me that if I found "parents," they would give me replacement brothers. If that didn't work, I had a backup plan.

During commercial breaks, I learned about the Rescue Ranch. The people who ran it were pighearted. Like me. The pigs were mayors and the people were butlers. The pigs don't get a whole giant room with cable TV and premium channels for only fourteen dollars a month, but they're not sandwiched or blanketed.

The lady at the Rescue Ranch was named Emily. She got promoted from head butler to Fairy Hogmother Saint. She has a buzz cut and a beautiful tattoo. She was a human lady, but besides that little detail, she looked just like me. That made her trustworthy. If I couldn't find new brothers, I'd find her so she could break me out of here. I was starting to get desperate.

The more I thought about it, the more I realized that my brothers were the forever kind of gone. Jeremiah Five probably wasn't asleep, and I was next. But who would come save me? I would have to do what the commercial said: "Call the Rescue Ranch and help save an animal today!" I was planning to work up the courage, but then Dr. Willis had a surprise for me: my very own people. They weren't dressed like butlers or doctors. I didn't want to get too hopeful, but when I looked up and saw the bald head of opportunity, I knew it was my turn. My chance to escape.

I listened to my pigheartedness and I could hear it: *family.*

The bald head was on top of my very own personal new dad. The exact kind that would get me a new brother. Dr. Willis also brought a short woman with brown-and-gray hair. She looked older than Dr. Willis, and her skin was much lighter. She must be Mom. Dad was skinny and had even less hair than Fairy Hogmother Saint Emily. His head reminded me of the rich man in the orphanage movie. He adopts the dancing kid. That meant I needed to dance.

It's a hard-knock life for me, I am a pig, you see. I couldn't remember the words to the song, but it didn't matter because they only heard oinking. I made up for it with my moves. It was time for my hams to shine.

"What's wrong with the pig? Is it having muscle spasms? Is it in pain?" asked Mom. It was a solid burn. I stopped dancing.

"He's fine," said Dr. Willis. "He's a little small, but he is our only success so far."

Darn right I am! I'm a success!

Dr. Willis kept going.

"I know that Jeremiah is awaiting major surgery, so I'll make this quick so you can get back to him. We have a problem. Mixing human and animal DNA is controversial, and it might get outlawed any day now. The bosses are ending the donor chimera program. Instead, they're pouring millions into new lab-grown hearts that don't require pigs. They would like to take Jeremiah out of the study and put him on the human donor list, which means he'd wait for a human heart. But, in my medical opinion, it would be more dangerous for him. That heart would be someone else's, and he could have complications. I still think the chimera, the pig, is Jeremiah's best bet at living a long, healthy life."

"Are you supposed to be telling us this?" asked Dad.

"Years ago, I promised you I would do everything I could to help Jeremiah, and you trusted me," said Dr. Willis. "But the decision is yours. You have two options. You can either wait for a human heart to become available or take the pig home and keep it at your house for the next three months until the heart is ready for harvest. Otherwise, we'd have to destroy the pig. It has a good heart, and I think it's your best bet."

Wait, destroy the pig? What are they talking about?

"Are we even allowed to do that? Just take the pig?" said Dad.

"Gen-e-heart doesn't officially want you to, but you have the right to choose whatever medical treatment you want for your son. If they refused, they risk getting sued and looking like they don't care about kids. You'd need to sign some papers and take full responsibility for any, um, mishaps."

"I'm not sure," said Mom hesitantly. "Both of our families live in Florida. We moved to be closer to the hospital. We don't have anyone here to help out."

"One of you would need to stay home to make sure nothing happened to the pig while you're taking care of Jeremiah. Keep it from eating any meat or anything dangerous, like avocados. I already prepared a list. And, it has…antisocial tendencies. It's unusually intelligent, but it gets bored. It isn't typically an aggressive animal, but it acts out when it gets frustrated. It's been known to bite," said Dr. Willis.

"We'll do whatever we have to if you really think this is the best chance for Jeremiah," said Dad.

Dr. Willis smiled. "This will work. The pump should help Jeremiah until the surgery, but it gets more dangerous the longer he goes without a new heart. The right side of his heart could still fail while he's waiting, so keep the pig safe. And you might not want to tell Jeremiah the truth. He has a tender heart."

I'm getting a job as a therapy pig to help someone with a "tender heart." This is a job interview, and I am a medical professional. I'll do my job, but if they try to sandwich me, I'll just get on the next train to the Rescue Ranch.

"We can move the specimen in two weeks."

I was on my best behavior for two whole weeks. As it turns out, the people around here are what the TV calls cold-blooded murderers or possibly sandwich eaters who will destroy innocent pigs. I thought Mom and Dad saved me until Dr. Willis brought me the same blue leash she used the last time I saw Jeremiah Five. The same leash she used when I hid under my cushion instead of saving my brother.

Dr. Willis, buddy, it doesn't have to be like this! I'm fine. Leave me here. I won't bite anyone ever again. I don't care how much you guys poke me. You can pick the TV channels. I'll be a good little bacon, I swear! But all that came out was "Oink."

CHAPTER FIVE

BOY

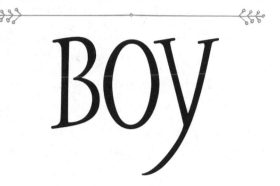

A beep knocked around my skull until I woke up.

I couldn't talk. A tube in my mouth choked me. Intubation tubes are like boa constrictors, except they choke you from the inside. I couldn't move. I ached.

The last thing I remembered was Adnan roasting me, then getting wheeled down the hall and going into the pre-operating room. It happened a few hours ago, but it felt like longer. Apparently, it was long enough for my mom to get here. She stood beside me wearing a mask over her nose and mouth. Her blurred hand petted my hair like a dog. She looked at me and looked away like I was her own personal sun. I hurt her eyes. This was my fault.

"You're so lucky," she kept repeating. It made her feel better. "It could have been so bad."

"I want a dog. Or a phone," I tried to say to distract her, but the words didn't come out. The tube caught them. I shouldn't have tried to talk. I coughed and a nurse rushed over to me. She shushed me like Mr. Walker during unit exams. I wouldn't have to worry about passing my classes this spring. Wouldn't have to worry about that week of stress. My mind floated off before everything fuzzed up and darkened.

The *beep, beep, beep,* woke me again. These beeps were from an empty IV bag. Mom hadn't moved. She said I was lucky. She meant I was lucky I didn't die.

I focused on a calendar hanging beside the sink. I stared at it until it made sense.

"My birthday is coming up," I wanted to say, but the tube was still lodged in my throat. I pointed at it. I needed to show her everything would get back to normal.

"It seems like the anesthesia is wearing off," the nurse said.

I caught Mom looking down at a big piece of gauze taped to my chest. It hid a scar straight out of *Frankenstein*. I tried to touch it, but my arms were tied up in tubes and wires.

Adnan suddenly appeared beside Mom. He wore a mask now, too. She jumped.

"Do you have to remind everyone about your birthday?" he said. "You would be better at fishing for presents if you were really sick. But you're fine now." He pointed to the vital signs monitor. "This line means you're fine. Boop. Boop. Boop." He didn't touch my nose, but he got his finger close. "Boop."

I gestured toward the screen. Adnan pointed at the flat line.

Without looking he said, "That's your love line. Sad."

Mom and Adnan left the cardiac care unit after I started laughing. Apparently, the nurse thought he was "too disruptive." It's the same thing our teachers said about him. Mom left with him so I could get a chance to rest.

Once they were gone, I remembered I was lucky. And that this was all my fault. I could be in my own bed right now if I did what I was supposed to. I pushed my head into the flat hospital pillow and tried to sleep.

The next two weeks were full of new experiences: I coughed up a plastic snake, went to the bathroom with an audience, saw Adnan three times and Paloma zero times, got tangled up in some wires coming out of my stomach, and learned I was a cyborg.

Then Dr. Willis knocked on the door to my room and said the magic words: "You're going home."

I was going to listen carefully to everything, understand everything, do everything she said. I wouldn't have to tell them I had ignored my ICD and knew I was putting myself in danger. I'd ask questions, just like Dad told me to. I'd get a new heart. All I had to do was follow the rules.

"Thankfully the ICD, his implantable cardioverter defibrillator, functioned like it was supposed to. The cardiac event was traumatic, but he is extremely lucky. There was still some death of tissue..."

Lucky. I knew that. I stopped listening. This must be how dogs feel when people have conversations with them. They can only understand a few words and have to figure the rest out. I'd been sick for my whole life. Until we moved here for this hospital, we used to have to drive hours to go to the hospital in Miami, but it never actually seemed like I was really sick. It seemed like a conspiracy everyone made up.

A part of my heart died. It sounded like a song lyric. I didn't listen to my heart and now it's dead. Even though I understood this, no one would tell me why I was trapped at the hospital. What was going on? I tried to listen again.

"Patients living with hypertrophic cardiomyopathy who are lucky enough to participate in clinical trials have had excellent outcomes," Dr. Willis said.

This was just like English class when we had to learn about hyperbole, and it was literally the most confusing thing ever. Why didn't they just say there wasn't enough room for the blood inside my heart?

My running during the soccer match caused the "death of heart tissue" and "lungs filling with fluid," but it could have been worse. Apparently, most kids with hearts like mine die before they know there's anything wrong with them. We had figured it out because my grandpa had it and passed it on to Dad. My father's case is really mild, but he had a fifty percent chance of passing it on to his kids, and I was the lucky one. Not Justus. Not Jazmine. Just me.

I wasn't supposed to have a heart attack; I was supposed to get my new heart as soon as it was ready. I had begged Mom to let me play soccer. Finally, she gave in, and I ruined everything. Dad thought it was his fault since the condition ran in the Johnston family. He didn't know this was actually my fault.

Dr. Willis turned to me. She pulled some pipes out of her pocket. They looked like she ripped them off a sink.

"This is your LVAD. It stands for left ventricular assist device. We placed it in your chest. It's tucked under your ribs, and it helps your heart pump. There's a screw inside that pushes blood continuously through your left ventricle and throughout your body."

She put her stethoscope on my ears. Then she held it up to her chest. I heard the normal *lub DUB, lub DUB*. Then she put the stethoscope on my heart. It barely went *lub*. No *DUB*. If I listened carefully, I could hear a low whirring sound. Kind of like I ate a tiny vacuum cleaner and left it plugged in. I felt my neck for my pulse. Nothing.

"This is your driveline." She opened my gown and pulled some tape back. A cord sprouted from my stomach and connected me to a machine. It looked like a special effect, and I really wanted to pull it.

"The driveline drives the pump in your chest. It's your power cord. If it gets unplugged, moves around, or gets wet, your heart will stop. It's your job to protect it. The driveline connects to a controller. The controller is the computer that controls your pump." The controller was the size of a graphing calculator. It had some buttons and numbers on it. "The controller is connected to these." She reached over to a table next to her. "Each battery holds a fourteen-hour charge. This treatment is your 'bridge to transplantation.' It will keep you healthy until your donor heart is ready. My lab grows hearts. We've been growing a heart for three months, but it needs to grow for three more months before we can harvest it and give it to you."

It all made sense. I needed to stay plugged in. I needed to be careful this time. It was all on me. Not Mom, not Dad, not my sisters. I had to do this alone. I understood. Mostly.

"How do you grow a heart? You grow it in the lab? In a jar or something? You don't get it from a dead guy?"

"Not really," Mom said. "Dr. Willis grew this perfect heart in her lab. It just needs to finish growing."

"Like a clone heart?"

"Yes."

"So, I'm a cyborg and I'm getting a clone heart?"

"Thousands of people have LVADs. It's just a tool to help keep you healthy. A lot of patients feel much better after they get them," said Dr. Willis.

I felt like I was being corrected. Like I'd said some thing rude, but I should be allowed to call myself whatever I want.

Then she went through everything we'd need to know. Throughout the rest of the day, nurses showed us how to take care of the LVAD. This was my fault. I killed my original heart and now I needed these mechanical parts inside me.

Dr. Willis gave me a laminated sheet of paper with magnets on the back. I wondered if the magnets would mess me up like the magnets in the electric pencil sharpener messed up the art teacher's laptop. It said everything I needed to do and everything I wasn't supposed to do. I wouldn't need it because I'd memorize everything. If I did this right, I wouldn't need luck.

CHAPTER SIX

PIG

I stopped before I took my first step out.

Goodbye, room 23! I'll never see you again. Never poop in your corners or get stabbed by your stabbers. Never, ever, never—But before I could finish, Dr. Willis yanked on my leash. All she heard was "Oink," but room 23 understood.

Room 23 was the biggest place I'd ever been. Then I saw a long hallway. There were probably five thousand closed doors on each side. I could turn around thousands of times in there. Maybe millions. I imagined the whole thing was full of brothers I couldn't save.

I thought the building housed room 23, the X-ray room, and then another room exactly like room 23 where the butlers and doctors lived. It never occurred to me that *room 23* meant there were at least twenty-two other rooms. It seemed like it took Dr. Willis and me about five years to get through the long hallway. Then we hit the outside door, and I was in for another shock. Dr. Willis pushed a metal bar. It was like walking on the rocky surface of the moon. I think. I hadn't had the chance to go to space yet. It was so beautiful. So much more than I ever imagined the world could be. I later learned this magical place was called a parking lot.

I forgot to be scared. The ceiling outside goes all the way up. It's called the sky. I've seen the sky in movies, but I could always tell it was fake. This sky looked real. It hurt my eyes.

I remembered that I should be scared. The sky was the color of my brother's ears before they left. I might as well be on the moon, naked, where any moon man could bite me, or the earth could fall down and smush me in a crater. I shut my eyes, and for the first time I liked the leash. It kept me from floating away.

I peeked through my beautifully long eyelashes that Dr. Willis says "are wasted on a pig" and saw a silver van with a ramp going up the side.

"I'll find you an apple, and we'll see if you can follow it into the van. Wait a minute," Dr. Willis muttered to herself.

I was a medical professional. I had a mom, a dad, and a job. I didn't do tricks like a puppy. Also, Dr. Willis never cuts up my apples. She gave them to me whole, and the TV taught me that I didn't want to stick a whole apple in my mouth. The Food and Travel Network taught me that putting an apple in a pig's mouth is dangerous. Dead pigs had apples in their mouths because it was "part of the traditional preparation for roasting and increases the aesthetic appeal of the dish." Instead, I strutted up the ramp, turned toward the front, and plopped my belly onto the floor. Dr. Willis closed the door and sat in the driver's seat. I could breathe again. Inside I couldn't float away.

I knew all about vans from TV. Vans are creatures that eat you and take you places. Their eyes glow and they wear shiny braces on their teeth. There are "state-of-the-art safety features included in every model," and about half the time you ride in one, the van would chase deadly assassins and flip over ramps until it blows up. That's what the "safety features" are for.

The "steering wheel" helps people catch up to shifty guys who kidnapped the president's daughter. The steering wheel is necessary for that because vans are not patriotic and won't save president's daughters by themselves.

Dr. Willis read the address "242 Ian Drive, Houston, Texas" into her phone. I didn't know we were in Texas. I vaguely suspected I might live in an underwater lair or possibly Russia. But Texas is fine, too.

The van had a buffet's worth of medical supplies. As a fellow medical professional, I knew all about these things. A thermometer hung on the wall. Its purpose is to beep and say a random number. There were several full water balloons that dangled from the ceiling in case a water balloon fight broke out on the highway, and finally, there was the poker. I have informed my doctors I am just fine with thermometers, balloons, and even icy Magic Tables, but I draw the line at pokers. Dr. Willis tried to distract me with an apple while she reached for it.

I knew what she was doing. She wanted to trick me with an apple, stab my dance machine, and knock me out. I knew better, but apples are delicious, and I hadn't finished my breakfast. I was too excited about the move. I lunged at the apple.

I felt a sting in my ham region.

I think I got stabbed again right before I woke up because the other cheek (not on my face) was sore.

Dr. Willis hooked me back onto my leash, and we stepped out under the too-big sky. Somehow, I knew my Mom and Dad would be here. I was home.

CHAPTER SEVEN

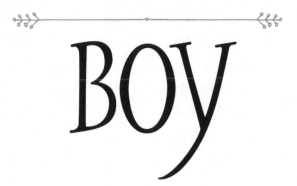

BOY

I went home the day before my birthday. The hospital sent me home with presents, but not the kind that get wrapped in bows. These presents were more like the ones puppies would leave beside the door: a wire sticking out of my stomach, a thick booklet of instructions, two smaller lists of reminders, a "home powerbase," four batteries, a long power cord, unit controller in a fanny pack, a harness backpack, and a new pump under my ribs.

The place where the doctors jabbed me was still sore. My insides ached like someone had been digging around in there.

"Jazmine, come here!" I said.

Jazmine set down a bag of green icing. The cake had

plastic goalposts on either side. She drew on a gumball with permanent marker to make a soccer ball. That was probably toxic, but Dr. Willis's list didn't say anything about marker licking. I think she was writing *Happy Birthday Jeremiah and Jazmine,* but I called her over before she could finish her name. I was born when Jazmine was four. I was her present. Now I had a present for her.

"I got you a card at the hospital."

She opened it and shook her head.

"A sixth grader shouldn't write 'Happy birth day *too* you' like that. It's like you're not trying. You just rush through without thinking. But what does it matter, it's just my birthday card."

"I was in the hospital."

"You're smart. There's no excuse for this. But thanks."

"You don't need to make me a cake." She gave me a look. "I saw the little bowl you got. And the spot in the corner cleared out. It's big enough for a crate. Am I getting a therapy dog or a regular dog?"

She laughed. "Kind of. Would you be okay if it was a hairless, chunky dog?"

I just got home and she was already messing with me. "Can you just get Dad?"

Dad sat down on the couch beside me. I checked Dr. Willis's list again. The list of symptoms that showed

I was dying and the list of things I wasn't allowed to do were equally long. I had to tell someone if I got shortness of breath or sweaty legs. Of course, I couldn't go swimming, but I also had to keep my legs straight. I couldn't cross them, and that was on the list. I didn't usually cross my legs, but now that I couldn't, I wanted to. Other things that might kill me were: sitting still in the same position, changing positions, not walking enough, or walking too much.

Dad seemed happy, like he had a secret he could barely keep. He crossed his legs as soon as he sat. Was he trying to show off? I didn't feel as bad for what I was about to say.

"Cancel the surprise party. I'm not ready. I can barely keep up with this list. Also, the more people I see, the more chances I have for infection. Shouldn't I be social distancing?" I was starting to sound like Paloma, who always seemed to worry.

"What surprise party?"

I gave Dad a look. Then the streamers. Then the big cake.

"It doesn't say you can't see people. We have another present for you. We have Dynamo tickets for November. Right before your transplant. Dr. Willis said we can go."

Twenty thousand people fit in Dynamo Stadium.

Twenty thousand germy people sneezing on me. Why would he plan something like that? I didn't deserve to go. I didn't deserve a party. Or an infection. This was up to me, and I had to make sure I stayed safe. No one else could help. I shook my head.

Dad kept talking. "You don't understand. When we told the Dynamo ticket office about you to make sure you'd be allowed on the elevator, they offered us free tickets. We'll get to go up in one of the boxes. You'd just have to wear a mask. The batteries will last long enough. It's three months from now, so you should be all healed up by then. The whole family can go. And your friends, too. They even arranged for you to meet that player you like. Andrew or Andre something."

"Andrés Rossi?"

"Yeah, him."

I thought I'd have to think it over, but I didn't need to think about anything. My list told me everything I needed to know.

"There, number seven." I pointed at it. "'Minimize risk of infection.' Please, Dad." They might as well be a bunch of zombies.

"It's fine, and I won't cancel it. Hopefully, you'll want to go."

"I won't. I promise."

Usually at this point in a conversation, a little voice would interrupt. I looked around the room for my little sister.

"Jazmine, you were watching the kids. Where's Justus?" Dad asked.

Not again.

CHAPTER EIGHT

PIG

My new home was like a house, but much worse. On TV, houses were tall, pointy on top, had columns in front of their porches, and "a well-landscaped exterior living space for entertaining" instead of a yard. Very calm lions and flamingos lived there. This place wasn't like that. Unfortunately, there was nowhere for the family's elderly booger-colored van to sleep, so it lived out on the street like a stray. The van probably ran off at night to go play with the other stray vans and get into trouble.

The front yard didn't look like much, either, but it smelled better than an orchard of burrito trees. While Dr. Willis was shutting the van door, I nibbled a blade of grass. So soft. So fresh. A little stringy, a little chewy, but still better than any pellet. Then, for the first time, I stuck my nose deep in the dirt and stabbed a hole in the planet. I breathed deep. The earth smelled better than the french fry Dr. Willis dropped one time, and it tasted even better than that.

A fairy creature came out from behind the only bush in the yard. It looked just like a replica of a lady human and made the noise I made when they tattooed me.

She was the first one to greet me. I presumed she was the loudest of the family, so she must be their leader. The TV had taught me that kids were the rulers of their domain, and the parents served them like butlers. The smaller they were, the more power they had. When they were the size of my head, they didn't even have to walk anywhere. They got carried. All they needed to do was scream, and they would get food delivered for them. I decided she was truly a queen, and so she was my equal.

As a sign of respect (and because I was too sore to break dance after getting stabbed in the butt), I curtsied for her. She gave me my first hug.

"You are beautiful." She clearly had excellent eyesight. She kissed me on the head and offered to take the leash from Dr. Willis. The doctor held on tight, not respecting the power structure here.

"I'm Jeremiah Six."

The queen bent down again and answered even though she only heard me oink.

"I'm Justus. Justus like Saint Justus except he was a boy and I'm a girl. My sister's name is Jazmine. And my brother is Jeremiah like in the Bible. He's twelve. And a mess."

Wait, what? Another Jeremiah?

"Justus, why don't you get your family?" said Dr. Willis.

Before the queen could go anywhere, the loudest scream I've ever heard erupted through the front door. "Justus, get your butt back in this house before I—" It was Mom! She transformed once she saw I was leading Dr. Willis through the yard. "Come on in, Doctor."

The walls were light brown and covered in T shapes and picture frames. A crayon drawing of a clown smiled up at me like he wanted a sandwich, but I could get rid of him. The rest of the house was nice. They knew I was coming because they draped the house in paper streamers. It was the kind of thing you do for honored guests like kings and Golden Globe nominees. It made sense. They were celebrating getting to live with me. I was very happy for them. I got to live with me all the time, but for these people it was a new adventure.

Jeremiah sat in a seat of honor. He was small, but at the same time he took up the whole room, like the light from the skinny lamp in the corner. He had a tan but no freckles and no smile. He also had hair like in a shampoo commercial. It was light brown and dandruff-flake free with luxurious volume and shine. I wasn't jealous, though. He must be second in command at this house, but a leash stuck out of his shirt and connected to a machine sitting beside him. If I were him, I'd want someone to cut me loose. Tomorrow, I'd bite clean through that thing. He'd be so grateful.

I walked toward him to pay my respects before my leash was yanked back on my neck. Then I noticed a taller, skinnier mom standing in the hallway. She wasn't with the family and had a trash bag in her hand. This must be the butler.

I felt a little disappointed that this Jeremiah hadn't turned out to be a pig. Poor guy. He didn't even get a number.

The doctor handed Dad boxes, went out to the van, and got a crate. The butler was named Jazmine. Queen Justus said Jazmine was a sister, which I guess means a girl brother, but she's mainly a butler. She walked over and seemed very interested in what the doctor was saying. This was because Jazmine was going to live in the crate. Good for her. At least she got to sleep inside. While they were talking, I took my chance to walk over to Jeremiah and smell him.

Ever smell a twelve-year-old boy? I wouldn't recommend it.

He smelled like what the butlers sprayed when I made a big mess, like chemicals and flowers. Why would anyone want to smell like that? Can't he roll around in the yard to make himself smell terrific?

"That's not a dog," Jeremiah said.

What do you say to that? Was it a compliment?

"Jazmine, please take the pig so Dr. Willis can bring the rest of the things in," Mom said.

Butler Jazmine took me to my room and shut the door for privacy. I needed a room. Getting a room meant I would get to stay. Getting a room meant no one would make me into a charbroiled pulled-pork sandwich on an artisan bun with a large order of fries and a drink included. My room was bigger than my whole apartment back in room 23. The walls already had brightly colored posters on them, and beside my bed was a huge pile of clothes for me to climb. I made my way to the top of Mount Pantsmore and leapt onto the mattress. Then I burrowed under the blankets. The pillow smelled fantastic. I couldn't help but nibble a tiny bit off the corner. Pillows look yummier than they taste.

I rolled back down my mountain and picked my bathroom. I considered pooping on a book pile, but that felt disrespectful. Instead, I found a soft purple-and-yellow-striped sweater to poop on. Stripes don't look good on me. I thought it was fine.

It was not fine.

Butler Jazmine opened the door and screamed.

She yanked my leash and dragged me out to her crate.

Butler, this crate is for you! You can have it all to yourself. I won't take it. My room is just fine. Just promise to clean it. It's a kidsty. A kidsty is like a pigsty but worse. She didn't get my joke because all that came out was "Oink."

Dr. Willis left and took the blue leash. I was locked up and these people didn't even know about my bad-boy past. There was the tattoo, but that's it. Tomorrow I'd start fresh. I'd make the best possible impression. I wasn't going back to room 23. Not today, not ever.

When I woke up, there was only one thing they could agree on. The short ones wanted cake for breakfast. Butler Jazmine made me something called "oatmeal with brown sugar, a dash of cinnamon, and a hint of nutmeg." I used to eat pellets, but this was much better. It was like if pellets graduated from the college of deliciousness. I thought it was the best possible non-burrito food.

While I was dancing and eating all over the kitchen, Mom took the cake off the counter. It must be a Pig Adoption Day cake. I followed her. I'd never tried cake, but it had a good reputation and was the same color as dirt. Then I saw it...

Oh no. Oh no, oh no, ohno ohno.

My cake was on fire. But it wasn't anyone's birthday.

Butler! Quick, do you see that! I screamed. *EMER-GENCY! EVACUATE THE BUILDING! WE ARE ALL GOING TO DIE! SAVE ME!* I kept yelling. I ran across the room and rammed Jeremiah's leg with my snout, but all he heard was "Oink!"

They were smiling even though they were all about to get sandwiched. Even though they were staring into a towering inferno. A vortex of flames. Certain death.

"I love fire," said Queen Justus.

GET OUT OF HERE! SAVE ME! ALSO SAVE THE QUEEN if you've already saved me and you have extra time, I said. It sounded like "OoooIiiiiNK!"

Jeremiah hit me with his ham-smackin' hand. "Shhh, quiet."

Jeremiah, I tried to speak clearly and calmly. Maybe this time he could understand. *Mom set the cake on fire. Fire will luau me. Also everyone else. Please listen.*

No one was doing anything. It was up to me. I had to be a hero this time. Once I saved them, they'd never put me back in the butler's crate. I would probably get the key to the city, a parade, and at least one federal holiday. Maybe I'd get officially promoted from pig to brother.

I knew I was supposed to fight fire with fire, but I didn't have any extra fire lying around. I looked for a fire hose or a dalmatian. Nothing. The only thing I could do was try to wrestle the fire until it died.

I slammed my head into Mom's leg. But she held strong. For a second, I wondered if this still counted as being a good boy. Then I looked at Jeremiah. He was horrified.

I'd explain it to him. *Jeremiah, only I can prevent fires! Me! Personally. I got this.*

I hit Mom again, knocking her onto her buns. I jumped up high in the air, did three flips, and came down to perform a perfect diving crossbody.

Either that, or maybe I just kind of tipped over onto my cake. I don't remember for sure.

Mom screamed in appreciation. Jazmine cussed for joy. I opened my eyes and stood back up. The fire was dead. I surveyed my work.

Queen Justus clapped. I bowed to her.

I walked over to check on Mom.

Hey, are you all right, Mom? I hope you didn't get burned. Would you like frosting? I said. My stomach was covered in it. She didn't answer. Even though I had to smush my own cake, I kindly offered her a taste by rubbing my belly on her head. She didn't eat it. I guess she wanted to save it for later. She did not say thank you.

I licked some of it off her face. It was almost as yummy as dirt.

Dad helped Mom up. Jeremiah said, "Call Dr. Willis. This pig's gotta go."

CHAPTER NINE

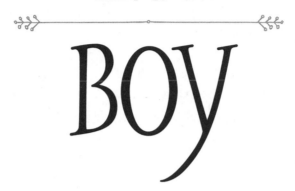

BOY

My heart wall woke me up with itching I couldn't scratch.
It's like the surgeons sewed me up with bugs inside.

I kept my eyes shut. I used to sleep on my stomach, but now I had to sleep on my back so the driveline wouldn't get pinched. Something like a slug crawled into my ear. Pig tongue. I jumped and my heart revved up. I'm not supposed to sit up quickly. I froze. I broke one of the rules on the list. Maybe my heart would stop forever. I felt more and more scared until I noticed a huge hammy face staring into my soul. Like he was plotting. I should have locked my door.

The bottom of his nose wiggled back and forth at me.

He made little noises that sounded like an evil croaking laugh. I couldn't spell the noise he made if I tried.

"Get out of here."

He backed away from the bed.

"Get away from my power cord!"

When I wasn't using batteries, my controller was plugged in to the powerbase with a cord. The pig looked at the cord, the powerbase, and stared at me.

"Muah-ha-ha!" he croaked.

He traced the path with his eyes, then nodded. He opened his mouth and leaned over. He put the cord that kept me alive in his mouth like it was a piece of spaghetti.

"Dad!"

The pig dropped the cord and turned his fuzzy head sideways like he couldn't believe he wasn't allowed to kill me.

Dad locked him up for attempted murder. I felt better after Dad helped me put in the batteries. Then we had to deal with the hole in the middle of my stomach. I tried to think of it as an umbilical cord instead of a worm burrowing in. At least it was always covered in gauze. Dad pulled the tape off. My stomach looked pale and hairless compared to my tanned arms, but I could feel the thousands of baby hairs getting yanked out. I tried to look, but that made me queasy. It didn't look like a part of me.

I peeked at it and all I could see was a human Capri Sun with a bendy straw. Dad put antiseptic around the hole and replaced the gauze.

The driveline that sprouted from my chest was just long enough to reach the fanny pack holding my system controller. Then, the batteries went in pouches in the arms of a backpack. The batteries were about as big as paperback books. This was my first day all suited up, and I looked like I was going hiking. Then Dad helped me put on my zip-up hoodie and walked me to the bathroom.

I froze in front of the mirror. I felt so weird, but with my hoodie, I looked just like I used to. No one could tell I had an LVAD. There could be people I used to see every day who could have the same thing, and I'd never know it.

I felt weak from the surgery, but besides that I didn't feel very different. Dr. Willis might have been right about this thing. Dad took my temperature and helped me onto the scale. Every day I had to weigh myself to make sure I wasn't holding on to fluids. He had to help me onto the toilet. I felt like a little boy. But I knew I needed him, and that was worse.

I hate needing anyone.

We used a grease pencil to fill in my temperature and weight on the laminated paper Dr. Willis gave me. It hung on the fridge now. I ate my breakfast in the living room since it was just me and Dad.

The pig refused to eat in the kitchen. He scooted his bowl onto the living room carpet and splashed his oatmeal on me.

"Go away."

Dad moved the bowl back into the kitchen, and the pig knocked it over and snorted. He had little ridges where eyebrows should be. It made him look almost like a person. He moved his eyebrows up like he wanted to say, *May I speak with your manager?* He was the size of Justus on her hands and knees, but his nose was stuck up in the air.

"Oink." He huffed at me again.

No one cleaned it up. He waited until the room was empty to lick the oats off the floor. Like he was embarrassed.

After breakfast, Dad put the pig back into the crate. He locked the door behind him. The pig snorted.

After breakfast, I went to my room. The door shut behind me.

I pretty much spent the summer outside, but now I had to get through seven hours of testing on a broken tablet I borrowed from school. It was covered in stickers and didn't have a camera. I could play *Fortnite*, but the microphone and headphone jack didn't work. I couldn't video chat anyone because Jazmine hardly ever let me borrow her phone. Since I'm now stuck at home, I really thought I'd get a phone for my birthday. I got one last year, but I dropped it in the bayou trying to take a picture of a perfect line of twelve ducklings. My parents swore I wouldn't get a replacement until it was time for upgrades. It was supposed to teach me "responsibility." Instead I had to use the tablet to message Paloma on Instagram. She didn't respond right away, but that was fine.

The second to last day of fifth grade, we had a community service field trip at a farm near the school. Adnan convinced me to tell Paloma I liked her. She ran away really fast. That's when I knew she'd make the soccer team this year. We didn't see each other over the summer and she didn't like to talk on the phone, so we messaged constantly. She usually responded by the end of the day.

Dad helped me with my exercises before lunch. Then I got out of my cage. I picked at a sandwich and only ate hot chips dipped in ranch.

I told Dad to feed the pig in his crate and not to let him out.

Dad let him out. He stuck his head into his bowl of

pellets and ran around the kitchen until the floor was covered in tan sprinkles. I went back to my room. The pig slumped back to his crate.

Around three, Justus got home and decided "both of the Jeremiahs" needed to play with her until my teacher arrived.

A different teacher from my school would visit every day. It's called a homebound program. Mr. Walker wasn't allowed in the house until he used hand sanitizer. Then he took off his shoes and washed his hands again. Even though a pig lived here.

Instead of going into the crate, the pig followed Justus into her room.

I peeked inside while Mr. Walker was getting ready. Justus had lined up stuffed animals. She stood in front of them, and the pig sat down where she told him to. She started teaching them the alphabet and which sounds went with which letters. He seemed to understand more than Professor Fuzzy Shark or Mr. Stinky Bear.

Maybe they could babysit each other. Justus constantly tried to force me to play "school." Why would I want to go to real school and then go to pretend school with an eight-year-old? I used to hide in my room as soon as she got home, but she'd tell on me and I'd get in trouble for ignoring her. At least the pig might keep her busy.

I walked back to the living room. Mr. Walker had been looking over my test results. The program knew when I started guessing. Apparently, I couldn't read at a sixth-grade level, but I could read Mr. Walker's face, and my future didn't look great. He made me redo four sections I might have "rushed through." I failed the others. He suggested working more slowly and reminded me of how we learned to find the lowest common denominator. I was pretty sure I was the lowest common denominator, but that didn't help me add fractions. Why was I so bad at everything? I just wanted to figure it out myself and do things on my own. I'd probably understand fractions if Mr. Walker didn't confuse me. After a pointless hour, I went back to my room.

I didn't open my door. I didn't finish the tests or redo those sections. I didn't want to check on Justus. I crawled into bed until Dad's knocking woke me up.

"I have a surprise for you."

"What?" I didn't move.

"Come on."

I forced myself to walk into the living room. Dad stood there, smiling, beside a wheelchair. I was trying to stand on my own two feet and my dad wanted to push me around.

"You're recovering and getting your endurance up. But with this baby we can go down to the bayou park. It's just a few blocks and—"

"No."

I used to love the park before my heart stopped on its soccer field. Every year we would go to the Pelican Bayou Neighborhood Food Festival. It's basically a park full of food trucks, tents, and music. But now it makes me sweat thinking about going back to the place that almost killed me. Besides, it was dangerous on its own.

Pelican Bayou is a slow-moving river with concrete walls. When it rains, the water overflows the concrete part and it looks like a normal river. The park is lower than the street so that in case of a storm it will flood before the actual street will, but it doesn't always work. The bayou was dangerous, but the next time I go there I'll walk. The whole world wanted to infect me and destroy my heart, and I was the only one who could stop it. I'd be safe, and I'd do it on my own two feet. One kid against the entire world is a lot. Just thinking about it made me tired, so I asked if we could sit on the couch.

"Mom's late."

"She picked up an extra shift at the plant because I'm

staying home now. I know you miss having her around more. She is the 'fun one,' but she'll be home before you're asleep."

"You don't have to stay home with me. I'd be fine by myself."

Dad looked sad while he shook his head. I could just tell that he didn't want to deal with me. He wanted me to handle it myself, but now Mom had to work even more than she used to. I wasn't even taking care of my own grades. I couldn't stop letting Dad down.

"Why did you let me play soccer?" He didn't know I knew I needed to stop. He trusted me to take care of myself, and I showed him I couldn't. I hurt myself. And my family. It was like I wasn't even really sick until I did that.

"Soccer makes you happy. That's important to me. We thought we could manage it safely, and we were wrong. But that's okay. Everything will work out all right. But I'm sorry you're stuck at the house and away from your friends."

Stuck with the pig.

Dad wiped my cheek.

"This isn't your fault. None of this is your fault."

I looked down. What he's really saying is, I can't do anything. He touched my shoulder and I jerked away. I wanted to hit him. I wanted to show him what kind of person I was. He loved working at the bank and had to quit because of me. But I wouldn't hit him. I wouldn't yell at him. He'd never know how bad I was. He'd just keep helping me.

"Some other kid might need the pig for therapy. Need him more than I do." Deserve him more than I do.

"No, he's just for you. I mean, it's just for you. You probably should just leave it alone. We probably shouldn't even let Justus spend too much time with it. Either way, it's just until your surgery. Then it won't be an issue anymore."

Why did Dad call the pig "it"? I don't know why his saying that annoyed me. I ate bacon, and I didn't particularly love farm animals, but the pig didn't do anything to deserve to get stuck with me. And he wasn't an it. He was annoying, but sometimes he seemed like he almost understood me. I decided the pig needed a name.

CHAPTER TEN

PIG

Don't move. I shivered. *Don't. Make. A. Sound. She could be anywhere.* I sneezed.

Creak. Oh no. What's that? Did she hear? Was it the ghost? No. The ghost haunted Jeremiah's room at night.

My heart, which Dr. Willis told me has a "superior vena cava"—making it better than anyone else's—thumped. I couldn't see the face, but the shoes gave it away. Sneaky light-up sneakers meant for style and stealth could only mean one thing: The queen was here. If she checked Mount Pantsmore, she'd find me and the game would be over. Before she could, she got scared. Jazmine could be back any minute. Instead of staying to fight, Justus left.

I'm the only one brave enough to hide in my room. No matter what Jazmine says, this is my room. I deserve it. It has been fifteen days since I moved in with Jeremiah and his family. If my math is right and I fully understand how calendars work, that means it has been about a month or possibly thirty-seven years since I got here. I deserved my room, but I still slept in the butler's crate. Jazmine stole my bed and wouldn't give it up. It was already bad enough being a pig that never gets to decide what he does, but they gave me a room and took it away for no good reason. I needed the room back.

First of all, the ghost in the wall of Jeremiah's room kept me up at night. The crate was right up against it. Also, butlers slept in crates. Pets like dogs or llamas slept in crates. If I slept in the crate, that meant I'm a pet, or worse, a butler. Brothers and sisters got rooms. I needed to get promoted to brother. I needed to get my own room. That meant helping the queen.

Earlier this morning, Queen Justus asked Jeremiah to play with her. He said no.

She asked to watch TV with him. No.

She asked to read to him. No. No.

It's the only word he knew. Some people don't respect royalty, and Jeremiah seems to think he's the ruler of his own little one-person kingdom. He barely sees the rest of us. So, I volunteered to play hide-and-seek. I was already acing her class. She had to promote me to brother if I did a good job hiding.

People are bad at this game because they smell bad. I mean that both ways. They are stinky and bad at smelling. Just when I thought I'd won and no one else would dare break into my room, Jazmine herself walked in. I was trapped. Dad followed her.

"Jeremiah seems upset. Did you tell him?" Dad whispered.

"No. He's lonely. We can't tell him about the pig. He'd do something dramatic. It's his only chance, and I think his heart might be getting worse."

"He'll hate us forever. All of us."

"I told him it was a therapy pig that can detect heart attacks. If he knew the truth, he'd overreact. Even if he doesn't talk to us for the rest of his life, at least he'll have the rest of..." Jazmine coughed and sniffed. She couldn't finish talking and left.

What was the secret? It was something Jeremiah wouldn't like. It felt dangerous. And it was about me. I needed to think of something. I needed a plan.

After they left, I snuck out of my room. Everyone had disappeared. I froze. The ghost was back. It wasn't night, but I'd know that ghost's sniffle anywhere.

I snuck up to Jeremiah's room. Ghostbusting would get me promoted to brother. I rammed his door as hard as I could.

GET OUT OF THIS HOUSE, YOU POLTER-GEIST! OR I WILL GHOSTBUST YOU SO HARD YOU'LL WISH YOU WERE HAUNTING ROOM 23! I shouted. But there was no ghost. Only Jeremiah heard me oink. The ghost sounds came out of him. Jeremiah himself couldn't be haunted. He is small and gross and doesn't have an open floor plan. He would make a terrible real estate investment.

"Go away."

He was crying. Perfect!

If I could fix that, then I'd get my big promotion. And I knew what to do. I needed to give him Butler Jazmine's phone so he could talk to Adnan and Paloma. Jeremiah complained that Adnan was busy and Paloma ghosted him. That just means "ignore." I knew better than to think that she was actually a ghost. I was smart enough to know that Adnan and Paloma were the tiny people that lived inside the phone. Also, I needed to get him outside. When I was in room 23 and I got to go outside, I felt better.

That night, I was so excited I almost couldn't sleep. Neither could Jeremiah. He cried for a long time.

As soon as the sun came up, Jeremiah walked over to me and said, "At least one of us should be free, big guy." If I were free, I'd get to decide where my feet went. I could listen to my special heart and do what it told me to instead of what everyone else told me to. Instead of setting me free, Jeremiah let me out in the living room. Mom told Dad to put me back in the crate. Dad told Jazmine. Jazmine told Jeremiah.

While she was in the bathroom, I stuck my head into her purse and took her cell phone. I was very careful not to bite and crush the kids living inside. I dropped an open yogurt in there, so she wouldn't be mad I borrowed her phone. Snacks make everyone happy.

Sunday was the day the whole family left us alone. Mom made us watch a show called *Church* on Jeremiah's tablet. Sometimes they called it *Mass* because the building is huge.

It was a boring show. There were no commercials and no fight scenes. None of the songs were good for dancing. Grandpa-Father Velazquez (Mom and Dad call him "father," which I figured made him my grandpa) stood at the front of the big room and read out of a fancy book. Words appeared on the screen. That was the only time I watched.

Queen Justus taught me there were shapes called

alphabet, which came in tall and short sizes. Each alphabet made a sound, or two sounds, or no sounds. If you put them together, you got words. If you figured out what the words said, it was called *reading*.

The problem with the alphabet was that the words were always in human and never in pig. The only word anyone ever heard was *Oink*. That's why I liked reading. One day maybe I could use the alphabet for human words and say something besides "Oink." But that was for another day. Today, I had a mission.

Jeremiah needed to go to the yard and eat some dirt. Maybe he'd be happy if he could finally poop in freedom. I delicately picked up Jazmine's phone and barely squeezed my way through the piggy door to the backyard. I used to fit, but now it's really tight. They must have gotten a smaller one.

All I needed to do was wait.

I almost dozed off in the sweet-smelling grass when I heard, "Pig!"

I jumped and picked up the phone.

"Pig!"

Call me Jeremiah Six. If that's confusing, give me a new name. Come here, and I'll give you the butler's cell phone. You will be so happy with me that you'll promote me to brother.

My oinks were messed up because of the phone in my mouth, but he must have gotten the gist because the door swung open.

He saw the phone. Without thinking he ran to me. "Jazmine will kill me, then you, and we'll get grounded. But I'll still get blamed for this."

He snatched the phone out of my mouth and put it in his pocket. He stretched his arms toward the warm sun. I looked at his bare feet. His toes curled into little fists in the grass. He breathed deep. He looked at the sky. He smiled.

Perfect. I dashed back into the house. I accidentally bumped the back door and it slammed shut. It clicked loudly.

I heard footsteps, but I didn't care. When I walked back by the hallway, Jeremiah's head was in the piggy door. He was too big to fit all the way through.

He couldn't reach the doorknob.

"You locked me out, dumb pig."

Oof. He wasn't supposed to say that. It almost sounded like I got a demotion. That's the opposite of a promotion. I went from Trained Medical Professional to Dumb Pig? But I helped him....

"I wish Dr. Willis would take you back."

No. She couldn't. I know I can't really follow my

heart now, but in room 23 I could barely even turn around. Plus, if she took me back, that'd be the end of me. I'd end up just like Jeremiah Five.

I marched over and headbutted him. He yanked his head out of the piggy door.

Go live in the shed, I screamed at him through the door. The roof of the shed was caving in, but he deserved it for his rudeness. Roofs are a privilege.

Somehow, Dad knew Jeremiah was locked outside. He came home right away and found Jeremiah on the back step. I went back into the butler's crate, and Jeremiah went to his room. I didn't hear any crying. I heard him talking to someone on the phone. For the first time, he laughed.

CHAPTER ELEVEN

BOY

"Don't name it." That's what Mom said after Justus called the pig Peppa. The *it* echoed in my head. Why didn't he get a name? And he wasn't allowed out of his crate except to eat and to go to the bathroom. The crate is meant for extra-large dogs, but it's almost too small to be comfortable for him now. He's a pig, so I guess it's his job to eat and grow. He's supposed to be a service animal and detect heart attacks, but how can he do that in a crate? I couldn't even look at him when his little eyes were so sad. He didn't deserve to be trapped.

At least I was free. The batteries made sure of that. Free to walk to the couch, to the table, to the bathroom, and then to the chair by my desk in my room. Free to let my big sister change the dressings around my driveline. I was free to do the exact same thing again the next day. And the next.

There wouldn't be a break. I told my parents I didn't want to go to the Dynamo game and meet Andrés Rossi. Even if I did, no one would want to go with me. Adnan's always busy with extracurriculars and Paloma still hasn't responded to any of my messages.

But I'm free. Free and alone. Free to break rules three, five, and nine on the list Dr. Willis gave me. I tried not to. I tried to stay in my room and play *Fortnite*.

I thought Jazmine's friend had already picked her up when my door swung open. "Have you seen my mentorship application?"

"No."

"What about the avocados? I was going to make guac to take to Stacy's. Did you eat them?"

Behind her, the pig snuck out from the back of the couch and eased into her room. His little snorting noises were quieter than usual. He was the last one I saw in the kitchen.

"Why would I steal avocados?"

"No. I'm not saying that. I mean, did you see them? Never mind, I..." Dramatic sigh. "Never mind."

"What?"

The pig snuck back out of her room and rushed to his crate. He'd never gone in there willingly. Not even at bedtime. He must have done something.

"Um." I pointed at her open door.

Jazmine ran into her room and screamed.

"Ugh!" She rushed out and got a text on her phone. "Stacy's here and I can't go. I can't leave that mess in there or the smell will never come out. This will take hours to clean up. I'll tell her I'm not coming."

I walked to her room. It was brutal. The pig either set off a green puke bomb, or he wasn't feeling great.

"I got it." I felt like a hero. "I'll clean your blankets, sheets, and floor. And that spot on the ceiling." Or ask Dad to. At least he could figure out how to fix her door latch.

"Seriously?" She acted like the pig had started talking. "Thanks." She smiled and moved like she was going to hug me, then decided not to. Instead, she left.

I stepped back into the living room.

"Dad, the pig's sick."

Dad walked over to the pig's crate and called Dr. Willis. I went back to playing *Fortnite*.

I'd just sniped Paloma's cousin when Dad popped his head into my room. "Let me know if it gets sick again. Or if it's acting weird. Dr. Willis said its siblings had some medical problems and we'd need to get it back to her if anything comes up."

Dr. Willis might take the pig just because he had one little accident? It wasn't even his fault.

As soon as the living room was clear, I crept up to his crate. He turned his head away from me. He never did that before. He didn't look at me.

"Outside?"

He perked up and knocked me over on his way to the door. Every time he walked or ran, he had to shake his butt. He couldn't stop dancing. I let him out and he dashed straight for the back gate. It was locked. He boogied along the edge of the fence and tried to nose his way under. He hit his head against the door of the shed.

"Oink oink oink oink."

It took me a minute to realize what he was doing. He was panicked and trying to run away. He froze when Dad stepped outside.

"How's it doing now? Dr. Willis says to call her back if it's acting weird."

"Oink!" His ears went flat against his head. He sat down. He lowered his head and shivered.

He was afraid of being sick. I couldn't let Dad know. I had to handle this myself. I'd save him without any help.

"No, he's acting totally normal. I think he's over it. See, he's eating grass. He's fine."

The pig looked at me and raised his eyebrows. I nodded at him. He stood up, lowered his head, and started eating grass. He looked up at Dad. Dad kept watching, so the pig wagged his tail, chomped some more grass, and started shaking his butt. That seemed to convince Dad, but as soon as he shut the door, the pig went berserk again. If I opened the gate and he had the chance to escape, he'd run off and I'd never see him again. At least when I was sick, I had Adnan with me. He didn't have any pig friends.

He ran over to me. He shivered again and nudged me with his leg.

"Oink," he said, but I almost heard, *Help.*

He ran back to the gate and pushed on it again. He scratched at the ground. He looked at me, at the gate, and at me again.

"Oink," he said, but I heard, *Please.*

I walked back into the house and raided the bathroom. I got five towels and threw them on my floor, filled a bowl with water, grabbed an apple, and rushed back outside. He didn't feel like eating the apple, but he followed me past his crate and into my room. He snorted as quietly as he could and spun around four times. After he found a good spot on the towel, he laid down on his side.

That night, I disobeyed three of the rules on the list Dr. Willis gave me.

I broke rule five when I didn't keep my legs straight. I sat cross-legged beside the pig for hours.

We binge-watched *Stranger Things* on Adnan's Netflix account. I needed to watch the pig breathe. Luckily his breathing was loud and oinky.

I broke rule three because I didn't sleep.

I watched him until I read on the vet website that he was probably safe. He refused my apple but didn't seem to be in pain. He rolled over, then back over again, like he was being dramatic. He kept tossing his head so I would pay attention to him.

I broke rule nine when I let myself stress all night.

Jazmine got home at noon the next day, and she was in a good mood for the first time in her life. The pig was feeling even better, and I was a hero. She even brought Justus and me a little bag of cookies she made at Stacy's house.

Having a nice sister was good while it lasted. About five minutes later, she sulked out of her room with arms full of blankets. I forgot to tell Dad about her room. I just said that the pig was sick. And I was too busy.

On the way to the laundry room, a paper fell out of the blanket heap. I picked it up and smoothed it out. It was the Gifted Students Mentorship Program application she was looking for, but it had some bite marks in the corner and a chunk missing from the middle. Sometimes the pig stares at papers like he's trying to read and then gets frustrated and tries to eat the paper. I understood that, but thanks to him I could barely read what Jazmine wrote.

I looked more carefully and noticed Dr. Willis's name. It made sense for Jazmine to want to shadow her since she was going to be a doctor. I turned it over to look at her essay on the back. *My first memory is also my worst memory. It was my fourth birthday, and it was the day my brother was born. The day he...*

The rest of the sentence was probably somewhere in the pig's stomach, but I'd read enough.

Jazmine got back to the living room and snatched the paper away.

"Where was that? You said you hadn't seen it. What happened to it? Now I have to redo everything. Ugh."

She crinkled it up and threw it in the trash.

She slammed her door shut.

I was never good enough for Jazmine, but I always remembered her taking care of me. Almost every day she changes the dressing on my driveline, and she's quick but gentler than Dad. I didn't know how she actually felt. The day I was born was her worst memory. She wasn't the only one that seemed to hate me.

I hadn't seen Adnan in a month and Paloma in longer. Adnan probably didn't want to deal with my problems, and he said Paloma was doing fine. Maybe she is, but she has left me on "read" for months. But I didn't like to think about that. Either way, the list said I needed to stay away from everyone to protect my heart, so it was all for the best.

But being lonely made me do weird things.

About a month after we got him, Dad went to get groceries at the H-E-B and I freed the pig. I did that every time Dad left. Now the pig expected it. I sat on my bed holding my soccer ball. I wouldn't actually go to the Dynamo game, but Rossi's autograph would look great on my ball. The pig danced into the room, shaking his tail. I wished I could hear whatever music he heard. He looked at the ball for a second then at me. He wiggled his eyebrows twice.

"Oink?"

He stuck his ears up straight. I was so lonely that I

dropped the ball on the floor and kicked it toward him. He spun around and whacked it back at me with the side of his face.

Before I knew it, we were in the yard kicking it back and forth until I got tired. I knew the pig wouldn't squeal on me. The next time Dad left, the pig found the ball and the same thing happened.

Most of the time, playing with the pig was Justus's job. When Dad caught them in her room, he put the pig back in his crate. Justus would either get him back out, or she'd stick her head in the crate with him.

One time, I found them watching the *Step Up* movie on TV. Justus bobbed her head to the music, but the pig stared with his mouth open. He got so close to the TV that his breath clouded part of the screen. When Channing Tatum did a backflip off a sound system, he tried to hop with his front legs. He fell over. He nearly knocked the TV off its table, but he got back up and looked at Justus like he was proud of himself. When he started shaking his butt to the music, I had to leave. He was too much.

Since I'm too old to play with Justus, I thought that she and the pig were great together. They usually kept each other from bothering me. But one day, they decided to change that. They burst into my room.

"Jerry, you have a problem." She said it in the same tone Jazmine used to yell at me. "You're sad."

"I'm not sad."

She rolled her eyes. She's in second grade, but she has attitude at a sixth-grade level.

"No, you make *me* sad."

I wanted to tell her to go watch cartoons, but instead I said, "Do I make you sad because I'm sick? And you feel bad for me?"

"No!" she screamed. "I've had it with you. Had. It. This is the last one. I'm at the end of my straw. The end." Justus sat down on the couch and grabbed my hand. "You are pitiful. I have more of a social life than you. Piggy said the same thing. He's more worried about you than I am. I asked him, 'What is that boy's problem?' He said you were a bad friend. Then I said, 'What do we do about him?' He said that you needed to have a party."

She used to be so sweet and cute. Where is she getting her attitude training? I looked at the pig.

"Pigs can't talk," I said.

I swear on the 174 dollars in my bank account that the pig rolled his eyes at me.

"Duh. Of course pigs can't talk." She turned to the pig. "Can you believe this guy?" I swear, the pig shook his head. She turned back to me. "He spelled it. Come here."

She dragged me into her room.

And there it was. Written on the carpet. Justus used her old blocks to spell out:

FRAND

And then:

PARTAY

"It's spelled wrong. You're in second grade. Didn't you already have that as a spelling word?"

"He just learned to spell. He hasn't even been to college. Could you spell good when you were a baby?"

I walked backward out of her room, keeping my eyes on the two of them. They stared at me. After I stepped out, Justus slowly shut the door but didn't break eye contact. They were still plotting. My arms exploded in goose bumps.

Maybe it *was* time to reschedule the birthday party. I'd invite Adnan. Maybe Paloma. Adnan tried to tell me why she didn't visit me in the hospital, but I felt like she was done with me. She could have at least messaged me. Leaving her out would cut the chance of infection in half and protect my heart a little better.

If Justus noticed I'm alone and made up a pig conversation about it, I needed to talk to Dad about having someone over.

CHAPTER TWELVE

PIG

There I was, minding my own business, when something punched the door. The house was under attack. Was I a vicious guard pig and not just a therapy pig? Was I ready for battle?

According to Justus, I learned to read in just two months. That's a world record. But that didn't get me a promotion. I learned to spell. That didn't get me a promotion. I'm BFFs with the queen. That didn't get me a promotion. Maybe the only way for me to get a promotion is to fight the door punchers.

Jeremiah was nervous about the invaders, too. He squirmed. "Dad, how do I look? How's my hair?"

"It's fine. Your shirt looks too straight. Like I ironed it."

Dad was right.

"You did iron it."

"But now you look like a dork." He did. "Scrunch your shirt up some, there you go. Okay. Smooth your hair. Perfect."

"Are the snacks out?"

"Yes, Jeremiah. With three fresh bottles of ranch."

"That's just for me, right? Wait, we need to hide the pig."

My own father dragged the butler crate into Jeremiah's room and threw me in.

I wasn't about to let invaders break into my house while I was locked up. I leaned against the side of the crate and tipped it over. The door sprang open. Then I nosed Jeremiah's door open. It doesn't really latch, so I was back in the living room in time to see a boy step inside and take off his shoes.

Jeremiah cracked a smile.

The boy looked at me and laughed.

"Before I came over, your sister texted me all the rules. I had to use hand sanitizer. And then wash my hands. And not get too close to you. I didn't take it personally. But then I come in and you're hanging out with the Notorious P.I.G.? Oh yeah, and your birthday isn't until next year, but I still got you something." Dad called him Adnan. He winked at Butler Jazmine, threw a present onto the table, and fell onto the couch.

"Now, I know it's just supposed to be me, but I didn't one hundred percent listen to you and got Paloma to come. I just saw her mom pull up."

A girl walked in a minute later.

"Um, this is for you. Sorry it's late." She set a suspiciously board game–shaped box on the table. She looked around the room so she wouldn't have to look at Jeremiah.

Then it was quiet for the next thirty-eight centuries.

"This is awkward," said Adnan.

Then Paloma said, "What's his name? Does he bite?"

"The doctor called him Jeremiah Six. He's just going to be here for a little while," Dad said.

Jeremiah leaned down near me and started petting my head.

"No, he's completely safe. He'd never bite anyone, I swear. Trust me. He's a service animal."

That's an upgrade from "Dumb Pig." I was almost a brother. I just needed one big gesture to seal the deal.

Then Adnan said, "If his name is Jeremiah, won't

that get confusing since you look identical and have the same name? If you really want to name him after yourself, just call him the Ball Hog."

"When are you going to get over that? It was just that one time," said Jeremiah.

Adnan shook his head and said, "Teamwork makes the dream work. If you're sensitive about your problems, we'll call him Piggy Smalls? Or HAMilton?" Jeremiah and the girl looked confused. So was I, and I am a properly educated professional pig.

"Maybe your name could be J6? How about that?" she said.

I liked it. The name sounded futuristic and reminded me of my brothers. This seemed like the beginning of a beautiful friendship. She even smelled like Jeremiah. I walked over to her to allow her the honor of scratching the itchy spot on my back.

She scooted down the couch and away from me like I was some kind of Jeremiah One. Why was she afraid of pigs? Had she committed a crime against pigkind?

She looked at Jeremiah. "I trust you. But I'm not so sure about J6. He might bite me because I had pork chops yesterday."

Wait, what does that mean?

"You'll like me way more than her. I've never eaten a

pig in my life. I won't pet you, but at least you can trust me," said Adnan.

She turned to me. "Fine. Sorry I ate your brothers. Just kidding. They were delicious."

Jeremiah laughed. I screamed inside. Did she eat Jeremiah Five? Was she joking? Who says that? That's not funny. I walked away from the zombie girl. I wanted to show her what it felt like to get bitten. Maybe then she wouldn't think it was such a funny thing to joke about. But biting people would get me arrested and taken back to room 23.

Instead, I stormed out. I tried to get through the piggy door, but it shrank again. If this family invites brother-eaters over, I might as well run away. In times like this, it would be nice to have a little freedom. But no. Pigs aren't allowed to decide anything for themselves. I watched them until they went outside. Then I crawled up onto the couch and fell asleep.

I woke up to a horrible sight. Someone's tragically skinny butt was plopped down a few inches from my face. It was Jeremiah. Gross. I moved back.

Dad walked out of the room while the brother-eating-zombie Paloma picked up some cups and tiny plates. She sat down between my face and Jeremiah and started scratching behind my ears. I got pig bumps, which are goose bumps that pigs get when killers touch them with their murder hands. I didn't hear Adnan anywhere. He probably left while I was sleeping because he is not a brother-eater and had the good sense to ditch Paloma.

Then she blurted out, "I didn't visit you."

"It's okay." Jeremiah looked at his knees. She grabbed his hand.

"No, you don't understand. Remember my abuelo? How he was sick for a really long time? Now every time I go into a hospital I cry and I can't stop. I actually went to visit you. I got into the lobby and all those old feelings came out. I couldn't go upstairs like that, so my mom took me home. I felt like a bad friend. I didn't know what to say when you messaged me, so I didn't answer. I kept feeling sick and horrible because I'm a bad friend. By the time I decided to reply it had been too long. And I've been feeling really bad about it."

"It's okay. I didn't know," said Jeremiah.

"I didn't want to come today. Adnan talked me into it." Jeremiah looked down. "I'm glad he did. And I'm so sorry." Jeremiah got Paloma a tissue. He sat back down really close to her. He gave her a hug.

"I'm going to be okay. I'm getting a transplant. Then I can come back to school. Now I can pretty much do everything I used to do. I can even take a shower if I put all of the electrical stuff in this special bag."

"Could you go swimming?"

"No. But that's about it. I can't dunk it in water or it might short out."

"Like that time I let you borrow my phone…," said Paloma.

"That was so long ago."

"And you dropped it…"

"Who remembers where I might have dropped it?"

"In the toilet. You're really not good at holding phones." She looked at him with an angry face until she couldn't hold it anymore and started laughing. So did Jeremiah.

"I was trying to catch you that Pokémon you wanted. The one that's a squirrel. Squirrelio or something? And I threw the ball too hard."

"The Pokémon was Eevee. But you don't have to make me feel better after I was a jerk. My new phone's better."

She showed it to him. Her phone didn't look like Jazmine's. The case had pictures of men with different colored hair.

"Who are they?" he asked. She got very excited and scooted closer to him. She made him listen to a song in another language. French maybe. Even though a murderer was trying to get closer to him, he didn't run away.

After the song finished, Jeremiah said, "Sorry I was

mad about you staying away. I didn't think about what happened with your grandfather, your abuelo."

"No. Don't say sorry. It's your job to get better, and my job to get over it and be a friend."

"You're a good friend. And you're pretty…good at soccer." He started looking around like he wished he could float away. "Wanna go to a Dynamo game? It's in three weeks, but it's on that Friday you don't have school. I checked."

"It depends. Who are they playing?"

"Um…"

"Just kidding. It's a date."

"Um, a date plus Adnan. And my mom. And Dad. And Justus. And Jazmine. And maybe J6."

She laughed.

"Paloma, your ride is out front!" Dad's voice called through the back door.

I had to interrupt. *Yeah, get out of here, you pig chewer! You can't fool me by crying.*

I oinked, but she looked at Jeremiah. "Is it okay if… I'm not sick or anything. No one in my house is sick. I looked it up online and it said…"

Jeremiah nodded. Then, she leaned over and bit his cheek. It was the worst bite I've ever seen. There was no blood, no screaming, she didn't even open her mouth. Jeremiah One would have laughed in her face. Then probably murdered everyone. When you bite someone, they're supposed to run away from you.

Then she leaned over again. I wasn't about to let her eat him. I imagined her biting Jeremiah Five. She said she ate my brothers, and now she wanted to eat my new brother? I did what Jeremiah One would have done. These jaws opened wide and clamped down on her leg. Maybe a little harder than necessary.

She screamed and jumped. Pork-chopping-brother-chomping zombies can dish it out, but they can't take it. She didn't even bleed. I think.

"Paloma, are you okay?"

She walked away from me, and halfway to the door she turned to Jeremiah.

"I hope he's not coming on our, um—"

I wouldn't let her finish that thought. I leapt off the couch and headbutted her as hard as I could. She fell, and I charged her again. She ran out the door.

I saved Jeremiah's life twice. I was getting my promotion this time, for sure.

CHAPTER THIRTEEN

BOY

J6 was desperate to ruin my life. He tried to bite my power cord that one time. He hasn't since, but still. Mom hated him, Dad didn't want him out of his crate, Jazmine couldn't stand him, and he made Justus imagine things. That would all be okay if he didn't hurt Paloma. He probably left a bruise, but I swore she was safe. She'd never snitch on him, but it was my job to make sure she was okay, and I let her down. It's more my fault than his. That meant it was my responsibility to make sure it could never happen again.

She trusted me enough to kiss me, then J6 made me a liar. It was like I hurt her. She'll probably never come back as long as he's here. She'd never go out with me. Never agree to go to the game. The only one that wanted him here was Dr. Willis. The worst part was how he strutted into my room like he was going to sleep there the night after he bit Paloma. He was *proud* of himself for hurting a kid. A girl. I threw him out.

He doesn't belong here. I thought about taking him to the farm co-op between my house and the school, but those little piggies go to market, and I only kind of wanted to kill him. While Jazmine was in the shower, I borrowed her phone and called the pound. They wouldn't take pigs. I asked them about pig rescue and they said I should call Oscar Mayer. I asked what his phone number was before I got the joke and hung up.

I kept googling, and I finally found Rescue Ranch. They saved animals from labs and were forty minutes north of here in Houston. I called them. I told them my pig bit a person. They said they had their hands full. They saved abused lab animals and rescued animals from natural disasters. They weren't a prison for vicious pigs. They asked if he was going to be "slaughtered." I told them no. They said he wasn't in danger so they couldn't make him a priority. They didn't know I might murder him.

He could bite Justus next. Or he'd bite me and give me an infection. I'd have to let him chance it on the street. He seemed weirdly smart for a pig. He'd survive.

The day after the party, Mom left me watching the livestream of Mass. She said, "Just because you can't be around all those people and their germs doesn't mean you have to miss out on the Word."

I waited at home until I watched my family arrive on my tablet. They sat behind Paloma. She hadn't gotten her leg amputated and didn't show any signs of turning into a werepig. That was a good sign. They're at church for an hour. No one would notice if I took a little walk. I looped the leash around J6's neck and dragged him out the front door.

I started up the sidewalk. I made it two blocks, turned down a street, then took J6 off the leash.

"Go away." I kicked at him, but he didn't flinch. I kept walking. I tried to ignore him. When I turned back around, the pig was still tailing me. I stared him down. He stared me up. I couldn't go home.

An empty Pringles can almost tripped me. I ripped off the lid and threw the can at J6. I was glad it bounced off the sidewalk and didn't hit him, but he chased it into someone's yard. He got his nose stuck in the can and swung his head around until he got dizzy and fell over.

I darted around a corner. I ducked behind a trash can. I escaped him. Maybe he'd never find his way back to my house. I could be normal. I could be free.

I almost jogged the next block. Going straight home was too risky. I had to lose him, but I was getting tired. I felt a little like how I felt at the beginning of the soccer game. Adnan goes to the mosque on Saturday instead of church on Sunday, so maybe I could stop by his house and say hi. The trip felt longer than it used to. I looked over my shoulder. No pig. After another block, the tiny incline that led to Adnan's house felt like climbing a slide. It started to rain. I needed a break. That's when the Oasis appeared.

The Oasis Market was a small brick building with a hand-painted sign on the roof and hand-painted tags on the bench underneath the window. I didn't bring any money. Instead of going inside, I sat to catch my breath and get out of the weather. I'd decided to give up on Adnan's house and head straight home when three kids, probably high schoolers, glared at me as they walked into the store.

I couldn't see J6. Maybe the rain made it hard to follow me. Good. Maybe he wandered into the street and got hit by a car. Why should I care? He poops on Jazmine's bed. But he also does bad things. He bit Paloma. He headbutts me. He's a stalker pig that won't leave me alone. And no one else will do anything about it. It has to be me. Again.

For a second, I thought about what Adnan said about teamwork. He keeps bringing that up. He keeps calling me a ball hog. I don't like it, but this isn't the time for teamwork.

I stood up and stepped into the road to see if I could spot that pig. He might have followed me. The sidewalk I'd walked down was empty. I thought he reappeared for a second, but then he was gone. I stepped farther into the street.

"Truck!"

I jumped and spun around. A pickup almost hit me. I caught myself with my elbows and knees on the ground and looked at the boy who yelled at me. He was short and had a scraggly mustache.

"What did you see, little boy?"

He didn't offer to help me up.

"I'm not a little boy." I climbed to my feet.

"What did you see?"

"Um, nothing?"

"Are you messing with me?"

"A Chevy? I think."

I looked around him and through the Oasis Market's glass door. The woman behind the counter had her hands up. Two other kids about the age of this guy were standing in front of her. I couldn't see what was in their hands. Then I understood. He was the lookout and his friends were robbing the store. He thought I was running off to rat him out.

"Were you going to call someone? Give me your phone."

"I don't have a phone," I said. My voice cracked.

I couldn't run, and the closest I'd ever gotten to fighting someone was when I got into an argument with the pig. And J6 always won. I needed to get out of there. At least the pig was probably safe.

I stepped back into the street. This time I looked first.

"Get back here. My friends aren't nice like me." The kid looked at the store. If I could just make it a few blocks before—

The barred door smashed into the wall as it slammed open and his friends stepped out.

CHAPTER FOURTEEN

PIG

When I finally found Jeremiah, he looked scared. I hid in the bushes and watched him back away from three huge guys. He tried to walk away from them, but they followed him across the street. If I left his body unguarded and something happened to him, Butler Jazmine would put me in a van and send me back to room 23. Jeremiah backed up to the brick wall of a building and they surrounded him. I'd had enough. I burst out of the bushes, I kept my mind on my promotion, and I cried out my fiercest battle cry, *Excuse me, sirs…*

Then I felt embarrassed. I'm glad all they heard was "Oink…"

The shortest one was twice as tall as Dad and had

an evil twirly mustache. The tallest one could have been the Statue of Liberty's fiancé. They didn't notice me. I backed up into the bushes.

"What was that?" the biggest one asked.

My well-formed heart with strong ventricle walls thumped and pumped and kept shaking. Now they were looking for the oinker. Save me, Fairy Hogmother Saint Emily!

The future Mister of Liberty pushed Jeremiah down. Mustache tried to hold him back, but Mister of Liberty went back for him. Jeremiah's head was on the pavement. He wasn't supposed to play contact sports. If he fell on his stomach...I heard the same sound I heard late at night when Jeremiah thought no one could hear him. And I heard my pigheartedness at the same time. Jeremiah was crying again. Jeremiah was a jerk. He might be the worst since Jeremiah One. He wanted me to get lost in this wilderness. He was rude. He was inconsiderate.

He's my brother! I screamed and rocketed out of the bushes.

"OOOOINNK!" I charged, full speed, across the street, into danger.

"What?" Mr. Mustache shouted.

BACK OFF, FUTURE SANDWICHES! OOOINK! OINK!

Mr. Mustache looked at Jeremiah, at the store, and then ran off.

"This pig's possessed!" said Mister of Liberty.

"He's got rabies!" said the other guy.

"He probably knows karate and has extensive martial arts training," said someone else (though I couldn't hear them properly). The door swung open again, and a lady ran outside with a cell phone to her ear.

"They're still here!" she exclaimed.

They looked from her, to me, then across the street at Jeremiah. Confused. They hadn't expected this pig because pigs aren't supposed to fight crime. I stopped before I bit them and gave them a last warning oink. They still weren't running. I'd have to fight them. I walked calmly forward.

I was almost in biting range when I heard it. The cops showed up. Jeremiah seemed just as scared of them as he was scared of Mister of Liberty. I ducked around a corner and Jeremiah followed. They got away, but so did we. Pigs aren't allowed to fill out police reports anyhow.

Jeremiah was a good boy and went with me all the way home. By the time we got there, our parents were at the house and calling our name. Mom ran outside and got in the van. She almost hit us backing out. I thought about how I never wanted to go back to room 23. How

I had to prove I was a good boy or my family might feed me to Paloma. I should just go right inside so I won't have to get locked up in the butler's crate. Then I looked up at Jeremiah and thought about how he doesn't like getting locked up, either.

"Don't pull another stunt like that again," I told him. All that came out was "Oink." I started running circles through the yard.

"Get back in the house, J6. *Now!*" Jeremiah screamed. He must have understood my oink. I tracked mud all over the living room until I let Butler Jazmine catch me and give me a bath. She yelled at me for running away, then she slammed the door of my jail cell harder than necessary. Mom was not happy with Jeremiah. Dad was a little proud.

That night Jeremiah broke me out of jail, and I slept on a pillow in his room. Our room.

CHAPTER FIFTEEN

BOY

After J6 saved me, he slept beside my bed. Sometimes he woke me up by snorting on my cheek, smacking his head into the side of my mattress, or oinking louder than necessary. I'd open my eyes and see a nose that looked like a mushroom guy from the Mario videogame inches from my face.

That nose woke up before the rest of him did. The sides of his nose flapped and stretched back and forth until his long eyelashes would flutter open. Every morning I'd sneak him back into his crate before Dad woke up. He still wasn't allowed out.

During the day, J6 headbutted me when I tried to slack off. After a few days, I would sometimes read to J6.

Somehow, he knew if I messed up. If I read the wrong word, he'd headbutt me again.

One day, my tablet said CURTSY, but I read "courtesy." He slammed his head into me, backed up, and kind of bowed. Like he was showing me how to curtsy. I realized that's the same thing he does to Justus every day. He doesn't do it to anyone else. Then, like a very confused person who forgot the difference between people and animals, I said to him, "You act like a pesky little brother." His tail started wagging as soon as he heard the word *brother*. His whole butt got the memo and started moving like it wasn't connected to his brain. It always did, but he never seemed to realize it. He tried to get it under control so he could headbutt me.

"Brother."

It happened again and I laughed. Maybe he thought it was his name?

"If you were a person, I'd think we were related. But you're just a pig. I shouldn't even be talking to you."

I tried to pet him, but he yanked his head away. I thought that the words didn't matter with animals, just the tone of voice, but his tail stopped moving, then his butt, and then a stillness took over. He looked around awkwardly and snorted. On his way out the door, he rooted in a blanket on the floor and sniffed at a stain on the carpet. He was trying to seem casual, like he didn't care about what I said. But was I actually being mean? How did he know?

The rest of the morning, I heard furniture scraping. I thought Dad got bored of the living room layout. At lunch, I found Dad staring at J6, who had lined up pillows and chairs to make a ramp. He was trying to sit in a chair. At the dining room table. Like a person. That night, before bed, I heard Jazmine chase J6 out of her room. Again. But it wasn't another pillow poop problem. This time he stole her hoodie. He dropped it on my floor and tried to crawl into it. The process was louder than it should've been.

"Calm down, buddy, you're fine just the way you are," I said. He looked at me and turned his head to the side. Then he looked back at the carpet like he didn't believe me.

"Brother," I said, and his tail started back up. He shook it so hard he almost fell over, and then he did a jerking kick thing he did when he was happy. After he wore himself out, he made his way over to the big green pillow, spun around, and fell asleep.

The next day, Justus announced she'd finished teaching J6 how to read. Dad laughed. I didn't even smile. Jazmine took a careful look at J6 and went to her room.

Afterward, J6 didn't go to Justus's room when she got home from school. He stayed with me all day like my own personal bodyguard. I missed Adnan and Paloma, but when I went back to school it would be weird to be away from J6. I started to wonder if he could go to my classes with me. I'd been researching more about pigs, and they're not technically allowed to be service animals, but maybe they'd make an exception for J6. And maybe I could take him to the soccer game in a few weeks. He'd be my wingman. It wouldn't be right if J6 didn't get to come. Animals are allowed on planes and in restaurants. There's no reason he wouldn't be able to. He's a therapy pig that thinks he's a bodyguard. A secret-service animal.

Saturday, I was eating hot chips on the couch. I'd dip them in ranch and catch most of them in my mouth. If I dropped one, J6 got it. If I caught too many in a row, I'd drop one on purpose. We did this until I ran out of dip. Before I could get up, J6 was in the kitchen and trying to get his front half into the fridge. Then came the crash.

He was almost covered in the margarine tubs Dad used to store leftovers. Only his curly little tail poked out, but he still climbed out of the pile with a crushed bottle of ranch in his mouth. He probably wanted to bring it to me and ended up biting down too hard. Since it was open anyhow, he set it down and lapped the dressing up like a kitten drinking milk. I would have been annoyed if I wasn't tempted to do the same thing sometimes.

Saturday is Mom's day off, and she was taking a nap. She's a shift supervisor at a Fresh Hill Farms distribution center and was on her feet all day. Usually a bomb couldn't wake her up, but J6 was a little louder.

She wasn't mad at us, just disappointed.

"I'm sick of these pig shenanigans. They're not supposed to live in houses. He's probably restless. Now how am I supposed to have pizza for lunch?" said Mom.

Ranch addiction runs in families. She'd starve to death before she'd eat a ranchless pizza. She tried to push the pizza off on me, but I didn't want any, either. I didn't tell her why, but my problem wasn't salad dressing, it was pepperoni. It's made out of pork. It'd been a few weeks since I could eat anything that had meat in it without getting upset. Mom would probably think I was being too sensitive.

Hot chips don't contain any meat, or any other nutrition, so they're okay.

J6 felt bad, but then he nosed at the back of the bottle. I ignored him and he headbutted me and pointed his head at the fridge. That's how I ended up making a bowl of homemade dressing for Mom. I had to substitute dill pickles for dillweed and onions for chives, but she seemed to like it.

Then I lost track of him. I searched throughout the house and finally had to resort to opening Jazmine's door. No one is allowed in there, but for some reason J6 used to love it. Before he started sleeping in my room, he'd park himself in there every few days. I cracked the door and the pig didn't look up. He had Jazmine's book open on the ground. It was one of Dr. Willis's college biology textbooks she had lent Jazmine.

He was looking at it and moving his head. Since his eyes are on the sides instead of in front, I didn't think he could see what's ahead of him clearly. He had to twist and wiggle his head at weird angles. Then he turned the page with his nose. It was so soft and flexible it almost seemed like the nose could grab each page.

"What are you doing?" I asked. J6 jumped when he heard me. He took off running around the room. Then he bolted for the door and knocked me down. I saw what he'd been looking at. The page had a Post-it on it and a highlighted sentence in a section called Careers, Biology, and You!

It said, *Research scientists at companies like Gen-*

e-heart International can take human DNA and inject it into the pig embryo. Using CRISPR technology, they grow human organs inside pigs. These organs have the potential to help patients live much longer than traditional human organ transplants. This exciting field…

I read it again. And again. I was trying to piece something together. Dr. Willis had other pigs? That she killed? I guess J6 was lucky that he got to live with me instead of getting his organs stolen. Maybe that's why we adopted him, to keep him safe. Maybe. And then it hit me. Was J6 actually reading?

I closed the book and looked for where it was supposed to go, so he wouldn't get caught. Then, on Jazmine's desk, I saw the new application she filled out for the Gifted Students Mentorship Program.

I set her book on her bed and picked up the paper. I turned it over. The question was, "What inspires you to pursue a career in medicine?"

I'd already read the first part: "My first memory is also my worst memory. It was my fourth birthday, and it was the day my brother was born." I felt a pang every time I remembered that. It was so hard to know that someone you thought loved you secretly hated you.

Then came the part that J6 probably ate. "The day I thought he might die. Jeremiah was born with a thick wall between the chambers of his heart and a hole right in the middle of it. I didn't understand what was going on, but I could feel a hole in my heart when—"

"GET OUT!"

I hadn't heard Jazmine come in.

I dropped her paper, and she snatched it back up. Her expression changed, and she shook her head.

"You read that?"

"Yeah." I didn't tell her that the last time I read it I thought that she despised me. She didn't. "Is that why you want to be a doctor? Because of me?"

She turned away from me and wiped her face. She took a moment, and when she turned back around, she looked calm again. She looked like she always did. Maybe she got upset a lot and was better at hiding it than I was.

"You know, Dr. Willis's dad died waiting to get a heart transplant. Now she's going to save your life. I can do that, too."

I didn't know that about Dr. Willis.

"More people are killed by their hearts than anything."

I'd seen that on a billboard somewhere: "Heart disease is the number one cause of death in America."

For a while I'd thought the dark cloud that followed Jazmine around was teenageritis. Then I thought it was her hatred of me, but it wasn't that, either.

"Be careful of your heart, too," I said.

I found J6 in my room, and he seemed serious. I tossed him a chip with the new dip, but he let it hit him in the face. He didn't oink.

"Good job with the fridge," I said.

He dragged a stack of jeans out of my closet and then got the board game Paloma gave me for my birthday. When I turned my head to see what the pig was doing, J6 pointed at the title of the game with his snout.

SORRY!

There were lots of explanations for J6 leaving that particular game on the floor. Maybe the colors drew him in, or the mildewed towel in the closet, but I suspected it was more than a coincidence.

"You're sorry?"

J6 nodded.

"Are you just moving your head around for no reason?"

J6 shook his head.

"Can you read?"

J6 nodded his head so hard his brains almost turned to cheese.

Justus wasn't home, so she wouldn't miss her alphabet flashcards. She used them for "teaching." I snagged them and spread them across my floor.

"Spell something."

First letter. J6 carefully stomped on the cards and bent half of them before his nose touched the first letter. He picked up the *O* and dropped it at my feet.

He walked back into the cards and rooted through them until he found the *I*. He picked it up and brought it to me.

Oi could be *ointment*, *oil*, and *oi*.

He waded back into the cards. It was getting harder because he'd wrecked so many of them, but eventually he found the *N*. Either J6 needed ointment, or pigs can't spell. I should have known better. I laid on my bed. I've been in this house too long. I'm getting cabin fever. Maybe I should be more excited about the surgery and going back to school. Maybe J6 would make me really popular. The other kids had cell phones, but no one else had a hilarious pig. For a minute, I actually believed the pig could write.

I shut my eyes until something bit my foot.

There it was in front of me.

OINK.

CHAPTER SIXTEEN

PIG

Jeremiah made me a word card. He wrote out the alphabet and a bunch of words on poster boards so I could communicate.

I'd gotten my promotion. I was Jeremiah's brother.

My excellent heart was full of happiness. I had a brother. I wanted to tell Jeremiah, so I brought three alphabet cards over to him. He smoothed them out on the floor.

"ORB?"

I shook my head no.

I nosed the cards around until it said BRO.

He wrote BROTHER and SISTER on the board. Then, nervously, I nosed Jeremiah.

I pointed to JEREMIAH-J6-BROTHER

He said, "Duh," and then hugged me.

"Since we're real brothers, I'm going to tell you something I haven't told anyone before. Is that okay?"

I nodded. I'm excellent at keeping secrets. Since I can't talk, I'd make an excellent spy. I am also very handsome.

"At the beginning of fourth grade, we still lived in Florida. One time, Jazmine was on her overnight Fall Trip all the eighth graders go on, and Justus was at daycare while Mom and Dad were working. That means that I would get to spend some time on my own at the house. They were always fussing over me, but since I was ten, they figured I could spend two hours at the house without a babysitter.

"I was messing around after school and had to run to the bus. I wasn't paying attention, and I ended up getting on the wrong one at the last minute. Everyone was acting so wild that the bus driver didn't notice, and I just sat there getting more and more lost. Then I recognized the grocery store we always go to, so I got off the bus at the next stop.

"I didn't ask for help. I didn't try to call my parents. I just walked home. It took about an hour and I went slow, but I made it home all by myself. Mom and Dad never knew. I'd never tell Jazmine, and I don't want to give Justus any ideas, but every time I have a problem, I think about how it felt that day I just found my way home. Like I got to be the person I really am. The person who can do things himself."

That made sense. I put my head on his knee. He scratched behind my ears.

"I've been trying to feel that way ever since."

I nodded, then pointed my snout at letters and numbers on the board. I had to tell him something, too. The most important thing. I pointed at: J1-J2-J3-J4-J5.

Jeremiah thought for a moment. I wished I could just tell him.

"Are those other pigs from the lab?"

I nodded. Jeremiah needed to understand.

"Your family."

I didn't have to tell him what happened. I could tell that he knew. And he understood why I didn't like to be alone. I'd had enough of that. We were opposites, but the same.

"I'm sorry. So, I guess, I'm like J7, then?"

Yes! Yes exactly! I danced my yes and he smiled back at me.

"I'm really sorry for how I treated you at first. I didn't know—"

I forgave him a while ago. I set my head on his lap and looked up at him. Sometimes, I needed the letters on the board. Sometimes, an "oink" was enough.

I knew my promotion wouldn't just be for me. Jeremiah's different now.

He'd talk to me all the time, even in front of the rest of the family. Usually, we don't even need the board. He pretty much knows what I'm thinking. And he's been standing up for me. No more sneaking me out of the cage. He just brings me to our room and argues with Butler Jazmine if she has anything to say about it.

But he still needs to see his other friends. Just one handsome brother isn't enough for him.

One day he said, "I've been looking it up, and I think that you're about six months old. That makes you an adult in pig years."

I had no idea. Six months. It sounded pretty old.

"I was thinking that I needed to get you something for your half birthday. What do you want?"

What did I want?

I wanted a lot of things, but no one ever asked me. It didn't ever matter what I wanted.

I closed my eyes to focus. I thought about grass

under my feet and in my mouth, and people everywhere trying to pet me, but I won't let them. Kids smiling at me and me dancing until they crack up laughing.

I nosed the letters on the board: O-U-T.

"You wanna go out somewhere?"

I nodded. Jeremiah needed some fresh air, too. We needed to have fun.

I was the first pig to get a half-birthday present. All because of Jeremiah.

The next day, Jeremiah burst into our room while I was napping. It was rude, but he was so excited I let it slide. Apparently, the Pelican Bayou Neighborhood Food Festival was this weekend. Dad even called Dr. Willis, and she said it was okay for him to go because it was outside. We'd just have to try not to get packed in too close with others. I'd make it my job to make sure that no one sneezed on or licked Jeremiah. He rattled on about food trucks and music, and by the time he finished I was almost as excited as he was.

Just a pig and his boy out on the town. What could possibly go wrong?

CHAPTER SEVENTEEN

BOY

The day finally came.

"Mom, I can just walk." I said.

"I know, but I want to make sure you don't overdo it. Consider this a trial run for the Dynamo Stadium."

"But what if I stand up and people see me? They'll think I'm a faker."

"Would you think someone was a faker if you saw them stand up from a wheelchair?"

"No." J6 pushed the wheelchair with his head, and it hit Mom in the back of the knee.

"I was so happy when you told me you wanted to go to the festival with your friends, but I'm really worried about the pig's behavior. Won't you be a little embarrassed of him? I mean, shouldn't he really stay in the house? For his own good?"

I defended my brother. "He needs to come with us. Please. I don't want to go without him."

Justus appeared out of nowhere. "Pretty please, Mom!"

"Only if your brother uses his chair."

Justus turned to me and made the most pitiful face I've ever seen on a human.

"Fine."

J6 and Justus danced around in a circle, and then he held perfectly still while she leashed him up. He understood the words I said to him, but Justus is the only one he'd actually listen to.

Paloma showed up first. She kept plenty of space between her and J6. I asked him to show some manners for once. His idea of being polite was to stare you down but not actually bite you.

"I'm really glad you're going to this thing. I thought I wouldn't get to see you until the Dynamo game. I got a special jersey for Rossi to sign."

After Adnan showed up, we left Jazmine at home and took off.

I wanted to push the wheels of the chair myself. I explained it was the least they could let me do. The two blocks it'd take to get to the park sloped slightly downhill.

I lost that argument and was in a bad mood for the first few minutes while Adnan pushed me. Paloma barely had enough room to walk beside us, so she fell behind to walk with Justus. If I were walking, the three of us could walk side by side without an issue. Instead, Justus was chirping and fluttering around Paloma like a pet-store finch. At least between Justus and J6, maybe people won't look at me. I hated that feeling. That's why I never used the elevator key they gave me at school.

It was only two blocks before we were waiting at the crosswalk beside a convenience store. I couldn't stop looking at the plaque on the doorframe: HURRICANE HARVEY WATER LEVEL. The plaque was about even with Dad's shoulder. Harvey was a few years before we moved to Houston, but I remember seeing the pictures on the news. The highest I've ever seen the water was where it flooded the park beside the bayou. The bayou was supposed to drain the floodwaters away from the neighborhoods, but it obviously didn't always work.

After we crossed the street, we had to walk about half a block to get to the ramp leading down into the park. I heard the drumline's performance before we could see anything. That bass felt like the pulse I didn't have anymore. I hadn't been back here since the heart attack, but when I looked at J6, I wasn't nervous.

We started down the ramp, and I was glad that we beat the crowds. I'd still have to wear my mask and keep my distance, but I'd be fine.

Before we got through the outer ring of food trucks, the smell of barbecue hit me. Even though I wasn't eating meat, my mouth watered. J6 sniffed the air, too, and his head tilted to the side. He looked up at me, and I patted him on the head. Everyone near us turned to look at J6, smiled at him or laughed a little, and then went on doing whatever they were doing. They didn't really care that he was at the festival. The people that brought their dogs pulled them in closer, but that was it.

It'd been a long time since I'd been around this many people, and seeing all those faces felt good. Then I saw something I didn't expect: a head of pink hair.

"Let's get closer to the stage," I said.

Adnan noticed who I was looking at and whispered, "Monica won't bite you. She's less dangerous than that pig." I guess Paloma told him. What else did she tell him?

"Monica's a jerk."

"And you're always nice to everyone? She talks smack and you're a ball hog. You're both terrible sports. Good job."

He had a point. The grass was a little tough on the chair, but when people saw me, they moved. On my feet I'd slip through the crowd and they wouldn't know I was ever there. Dad helped Adnan find a spot for me that was kind of socially distanced but close to the stage. It was near the fifteen-foot-tall pelican sculpture on the edge of the bayou. The upper beak of its shiny scrap metal head pointed straight up and looked almost like a sword. It was the only pelican I'd ever seen in Pelican Bayou Park.

I should've known that if Mom got closer to the music, she'd start dancing. She's like J6 that way. But J6 wasn't dancing. He had music and attention, but he was almost still. He shivered.

"Are you okay?" I asked him. His eyes were huge and more focused than I've ever seen. I tried to figure out what was bothering him, and I should have noticed it sooner. The barbecue truck nearest us had a big sign with a pig in a chef's hat and apron holding a knife in one hand and a sandwich in the other hand.

I didn't have time to warn Mom before he bolted. The leash was wrapped around her wrist, but he pulled her down and yanked it free.

He ran in the opposite direction of the barbecue truck. The crowd parted for him; some people screamed.

Mom and Paloma took off running after J6. Dad caught Justus's arm before she could join in.

Paloma probably wasn't going to be much help catching him. I don't know why, but J6 doesn't seem to like her and might run even faster if he saw her chasing him. According to the internet, domesticated pigs can only run about ten miles per hour. J6 is very domesticated.

I lost sight of J6 until I heard a table crashing to the ground, people screaming, then I finally saw him again. He ran straight for a Korean BBQ truck before he looked up at the sign, spun around, and darted behind a stall.

I looked around. J6 isn't exactly an athlete, and he'd get tired soon. He'd try to hide. But where?

And then I noticed a booth off to the side. It had a high sign you could see across the park: LOST AND FOUND.

"Over there."

Adnan gave me a look, but Dad let him wheel me over to the booth.

Around the back all I could see was a spotted light-pink butt and a terrified tail.

CHAPTER EIGHTEEN

PIG

Aside from narrowly escaping getting turned into a "pulled-pork sandwich on an artisan bun with a large order of fries and drink included," life was perfect. My pigheartedness felt complete and I had a brother.

Butlers can go away. Pets can go away. Brothers are forever.

No one told the butler. The next afternoon, Jazmine put me back in the crate. I tried to tell her I got a promotion, but she didn't understand. Maybe she was jealous.

"Do you think the pig is acting weird? I knew that walk to the festival was a bad idea," she whispered to Dad in the kitchen.

Dad laughed and said, "Dr. Willis said the trip was

okay. It really cheered Jeremiah up. We only have to put up with him for another week. Actually, Dr. Willis is going to come get him while we're at the soccer game. If Jeremiah and Justus were home, they'd throw a fit. They're getting kind of attached. I guess I dropped the ball on keeping them all separated. They'll miss him. I will, too."

Jazmine shushed him and looked at me.

After Jeremiah let me out, I ran to my word card. I touched: JAZMINE-SAID-J6-GO-SOCCER.

"You can go to the game?"

No.

Jeremiah flipped the card over to the new alphabet board he made me. I nosed P-I-G-N-A-P and touched the words DOCTOR-TIME-SOCCER. I wanted to scream, *She will sandwich me.*

"You are not making sense. Next week is the soccer game?"

BAD-DOCTOR-HURT-PIG.

"I'll ask her about you when I see her Wednesday. Just, uh, be good, I guess?"

I left room 23 to move here, and from day one the only thing I wanted to do was be a good boy and get my promotion. But they still don't want me. I saved them from the cake and the zombie girl. But it wasn't enough.

Maybe I could be so good that Butler Jazmine and Dad would change their minds? Maybe I could be perfect.

∾

The next morning, I snuck out of our room early to make everyone breakfast. The bowls and cereal were on the bottom shelf so Justus could reach them. Same for the milk. I did a great job and only smashed three bowls. Jazmine didn't give me the chance to clean up when she exploded out of her room and screamed at me. The milk jug fell, bounced off the table, and poured onto the ground. For breakfast, all I got was the piece of banana Justus slipped me through the bars of the butler's crate.

When they were alone for a minute, Dad told Jazmine, "He'll be gone soon."

Everything I did made it worse. I tried to get my mind quiet and listen to my pigheartedness, but I couldn't hear anything. My insides were screaming and every part of me was afraid. The worst part was that Jeremiah didn't understand what was happening. Or he didn't care.

Did Jeremiah Five know that I cared when he got taken away? I didn't save him, either. He loved me, and I didn't protect him. Now the same thing was going to happen to me.

Pigs never get to decide anything for themselves.

Everyone decides what to do with us. They lock us up, eat us, cut us up—it doesn't matter. They'll do it right in the middle of a park and no one cares.

What can one little pig do?

My head hurt. I've been trapped since room 23. I thought I got out, but I didn't.

For the first time in my life I actually screamed, and for the first time in my life I sounded like a person. If I screamed loud enough maybe someone that cared would hear me.

Jazmine didn't even leave her room. She just yelled "Shut up" through the door.

I did.

Jeremiah rushed out of his room. He looked distracted.

"Is everything okay?" he asked.

I gave him a withering look. If he were my real brother, he'd know that everything was not okay. Instead, he just patted me through the wires and went back to his room.

That meant my time here was up. It didn't matter that I got promoted. It didn't matter that I wanted to be Jeremiah's brother. My heart used to be "perfectly formed and fully functional," but now it was broken. I'd wait to see what Jeremiah had to say, but it looked like I was going to have to finally decide something for myself. It was time to run away. I was going to the Rescue Ranch.

CHAPTER NINETEEN

BOY

I sat on Dr. Willis's papered table and stared at the framed pictures she had of her and her mom at graduation. Her dad wasn't there, and I felt bad for her. Dr. Willis wasn't evil back then. She had a huge smile and long braids and looked too young to graduate. Her long hair and happiness were gone, but she still looked younger than thirty.

She found us when I was ten. That's when we left Florida, left our whole family, and moved to Houston. She'd been hunting for the perfect victim to save. That was the first time I heard I was lucky. Jazmine said finding Dr. Willis was like winning the lottery. I was lucky because my heart was sick enough to need a transplant. Lucky because the doctor discovered my heart problems when I was born. Lucky that I got an ICD. Lucky that I got an LVAD just before my heart was ready.

I'd been curious about Gen-e-heart since I read that section in Jazmine's book. I didn't want to think about it. I didn't want to believe that they were planning on stealing J6's heart for me. I had just about put it out of my mind when J6 freaked out the other day. I guess I was lucky that J6 had a perfect heart for me. Lucky.

Dr. Willis said I was part of a clinical trial, but it felt like J6 was on trial and ended up on death row. All because of me. Her office was always cold, but now her hands made me shiver before they touched my back.

"Guess who's the lucky kid that gets to go back to school in a few months?" she asked. Dr. Willis was acting like a new teacher. She got extra cheerful when no one wanted anything to do with her. "The heart is ready for you. The doctors need to make some preparations, but that's it. You just need to take it easy. Only walk short distances. The LVAD helps the left side of your heart, but the right side is getting worn out. Going to the park with your family was fine, and you can still go to the Dynamo game on Friday unless it gets rained out. Then you'll come in on Saturday and we'll operate Monday!"

She moved her stethoscope to a different part of my back. Probably looking for the best place to stab me.

"Breathe in. Hold it. And out."

But maybe J6 heard wrong. Maybe I misinterpreted what he was trying to tell me. I prayed she would tell me everything was going to be okay.

"I have questions about the pig," I said.

"You can breathe normally. What's your question?"

I took a deep breath.

"He isn't like a regular pig, is he?"

"Um, no. He's a chimera. I guess they told you that's what Gen-e-heart researches. What else did your family tell you?"

I squirmed and the paper under me crinkled. She wanted to know what I already knew. She wanted to lie to me. I could lie just as well as she could.

"Dad told me his heart is, um, for my transplant."

She actually smiled, relieved. "Exactly! That's what the clinical trial is about. We made him special for you. We cut out some of his genes before he was born. Then we gave him some of the stem cells we harvested from your skin cells. He's specially designed to help you. Is this what you're nervous about?"

That's exactly what Jazmine's book said. I didn't want to believe it. I needed to say something, but I couldn't. I turned my head away. I couldn't leave. Is this how J6 felt before he got to move in with me? I wanted to rush out the door and scream. I wanted to hit someone.

I wiped my eye.

"Jeremiah, you're shaking. Are you okay?"

"Yeah."

"I understand that you're afraid of surgery. This won't be much worse than the surgery for your cardioverter or the LVAD. You know what? Some kids with other heart conditions have had to have dozens of surgeries. You've had lots of checkups, some restrictions on your activities, but your third surgery might be your last one. I will do everything I can to keep you safe. You really are lucky."

I turned my head farther. She didn't care if I was okay. Sometimes when I got angry enough, I cried. I hated that. It was like my feelings were making fun of me. Like I was calling myself a baby. My prayer didn't work. This could have been another time J6 got confused. It could have been another birthday cake incident. I thought I'd go home and laugh about it with him. She said she'd take care of me, but she was going to kill J6.

Premeditated murder. To her, J6 was just like all of the other pigs in the world. Except…

"You're breathing a little fast. Go ahead and breathe like you normally would."

How did I usually breathe? I sucked in a breath and held it for three seconds.

"If the pig can have a human heart…" I stopped to breathe because my voice was about to crack. I still wasn't looking at her. "Could you have messed up and given him a human brain? Could you have made him too human?"

This was my fault. He was going to die because I got sick. It should be me.

"With new medical procedures there's always the risk of unintended side effects, but what you're talking about is unlikely. Don't worry. If he had a human brain, you'd know it."

"Are you sure we have to use that heart? Is there another option?"

She looked concerned. "Sorry, but there really isn't. We're ending the donor chimera program, and we've developed a lab-grown heart that doesn't use any pigs, but it's too experimental."

"That's really interesting." I tried to look curious.

Dr. Willis grinned and took out her phone, "I love it when kids are interested in science. Here's the proto-type." She showed me a video of a heart in a glass cylinder attached to wires and tubes. It was beating. Dr. Willis was a mad scientist. "Of course, it's still in animal trials now. I'd have to know it was safe for humans before I tried it on you. You're the most important thing. This Monday, you get a heart. By then, it'll all be over."

"Okay."

She opened the door for me, and I put my hands over my face. I ugly cried and felt my throat and upper lip twitch. I made it to the bathroom in time to throw up. I washed my mouth out and wiped my tongue with a paper towel. I dabbed my eyes so they wouldn't puff up, but they were still red. I wished I could take some toilet paper and scrub them until they turned white. Dad couldn't find out I knew his plan. If he knew, he'd change it. If he changed the plan, J6 didn't have a chance.

He wouldn't make it until Christmas. Not even Thanksgiving. I counted the days on my fingers. Today, then Thursday, Friday, Saturday, Sunday, and Monday. He had six days to live. How would I tell him he had six days to live? What would I do?

When I got to the waiting room, Dad smiled at me.

"I forgot; I need to give Dr. Willis something."

He was going to leave me in the waiting room and find her, but she found him first. She turned her back to me, but I saw Dad fish something out of his pocket. I heard the jangle of keys. I saw Dr. Willis pocket what she gave him. It seemed like Dad was letting Dr. Willis steal J6 while I was at the soccer game. But Dad would never do that to me.

Or at least that's what I thought until Dad turned around, looked at me for a second, and looked away. He looked ashamed.

"How would you feel about stopping for ice cream?"

I didn't answer him. It wasn't my job to make him feel better about lying to me. I looked away and followed him to the parking lot. Getting into the van with Dad felt like getting kidnapped. I didn't know this guy. I thought I did, but the Dad I knew my whole life wouldn't do this. My dad wouldn't plan a murder.

He tried to talk to me.

"I think it's time we really start thinking about getting a dog. Maybe after the transplant? Not a service dog, either. A destroy-everything, shed-all-over-the-house, pain-in-the-butt dog."

"Yeah." He didn't know I knew, but the last thing I wanted to do was talk to him.

"Think about it. We can check out the shelter web-sites while you're recovering in the hospital."

I couldn't answer him because I wasn't sure I could control what I said. I stared through the ghost of my face in the window and tuned out the radio's tropical storm news. Traffic stopped on the bridge over Pelican Bayou just like it always did. I stared at the scrap metal pelican sculpture with its beak higher than the trees planted after Hurricane Harvey. The pelican looked like it wanted to fly, but it couldn't. J6 knew how it felt to be bolted to the ground. He was supposed to stay put until Dr. Willis decided he would die. It wasn't right.

I turned to look at the top of Dynamo Stadium peeking out at me from between the buildings. In two days, I was supposed to meet Andrés Rossi and then come home to an empty house.

At least, that's what my family planned.

CHAPTER TWENTY

PIG

According to Jazmine, with all her years of butler knowledge, Dr. Willis will pignap me in two days.

I understood Jazmine's book now. It meant that the doctor will rip my heart out and stick it in my brother. I had less than one week to live. Less than one week to come up with a plan that will make sure Jeremiah gets a new heart that nobody is using. Less than one week to save us both.

Meanwhile, Jeremiah was taking his sweet time finding the truth. Why wasn't he home yet? Did he stop for pizza? Did Dad's van explode? This could be my last Wednesday, and my brother couldn't be bothered to hurry home.

At least Queen Justus let me out of the butler crate so I could be by the door as soon as he got back. These were precious seconds I didn't have to waste and worry. Finally, after sixty-six million years, the door swung open and bonked me in the head.

For the first time, Dad said, "Sorry." He gave me a sad look and walked through the living room.

At last, Jeremiah came in. It would hurt to find out the truth, but it was better than waiting. Either way, I had to know so we could come up with our backup plan. I stood in front of him and turned my head to the side. I perked my ears so he'd know I was ready to listen.

He looked like he had just eaten a bunch of avocados and was about to make a mess of Butler Jazmine's blankets. He pushed the front door, but he didn't bother making sure that it actually closed. He stepped around me and went to the bathroom.

I followed him to the door. He was quiet in there. Not sick. Almost like he wanted to be by himself.

What did you find out? There's got to be a way for both of us. We just need to think about it, I asked through the locked door. I should've waited until we were face-to-face, but I didn't have any time.

He answered my "Oink" with a whisper: "Not now."

When he finished up, he opened the door and said, "Don't follow me. I need to think."

He looked like he was hurting. How am I supposed to leave him like that?

I pretended like I was going to sit in front of the TV but turned at the last minute and followed him to our room. He wasn't paying attention and slammed the door so hard that for the second time today, I got hit. This time it got me in the nose. I smelled blood before I tasted it, but my face didn't hurt as much as my heart did.

This is an emergency. What do I do? I need your help and you need mine. I'm your brother. We don't have time for this. Please!

I turned to Justus. She shrugged. I walked over to her and nudged her with my achy nose until she opened our door for me. Jeremiah was lying on his bed. He didn't care that the door hit me. His face looked like he didn't care about anything, not even my impending sandwichness.

I headbutted him.

He finally spoke up, but he didn't look at me. He didn't move. "Dr. Willis is probably going to try to take you during the soccer game Friday. I need to think. Give me time."

Time? I don't have time! I paced around the room

and knocked some books off the shelf. I was a Popsicle melting in the sun, and he was acting like there wasn't any reason to panic.

I turned to him and snorted as loud and as growly as I could. The only problem is that pig growls sound like puppies crying. It's a tough fact to face, but I'm just too adorable. It's my curse. He wasn't even a little intimidated.

Butler Jazmine threw open the door. She didn't knock. That's rude and unacceptable behavior because Jeremiah and I were in the middle of a very important conversation, and I didn't give her permission to interrupt. Also, butlers are always supposed to knock. Ask Batman.

Hey! I said. All that came out was "Oink," but that didn't matter because she wasn't listening anyway. Her phone was by her ear.

"It's for you," she said to Jeremiah because she always ignored me.

"I'm not here."

"He says he's not here, *Paloma*," said Jazmine. She looked at him when she said the zombie girl's name, and Jeremiah sat up.

"Give it!"

He wanted to talk to the killer who tried to eat him

and might have eaten my brothers. Then, while I was trying to avoid getting sandwiched at the "neighborhood festival," she chased me. Probably because she was hungry. I gave him a look to show him how disappointed I was with his behavior today.

He caught the phone and held it to his ear. He took a long time to answer questions. Eventually, I pieced a sentence together.

"I'm fine.... Friday?...The plan?" He looked at me, "We're still going to the game. For sure."

I headbutted him again. If this was some kind of scheme, he needed to tell me. If it was a lie, all he would have to do was wink or shake his head. Instead, he shooed me away. Like he didn't care. Like I was nothing. I wanted to say something to him, but for the first time nothing came out. Not even an oink. What could I say? His silence was my answer.

I rushed out of our room so fast I almost knocked Jazmine down. She smacked me on the head. I ran down the hall and almost tripped Dad. He yelled at me and tried to catch me. My very strong heart with strong ventricle walls beat so fast I could feel it. Finally, Dad tackled me and chucked me into the butler crate.

I don't sleep here anymore! I got a promotion! He only heard "Oink," but he wouldn't have cared even if he understood. He went back to his room. I rammed the side. They must have gotten a tinier crate because I barely had any room to build up speed. I leaned against the side and let it roll over. One of the wire clasps popped loose, and the crate collapsed around me. I fought my way to freedom.

If we worked together, we could find a way to save both of us. We'd find a different heart, because I needed mine. But he didn't want to figure it out. He didn't even want to try.

I gave my brother my heart. He just gave up.

I guess he never really cared. When did Jeremiah change his mind about me? Was it when he found what my heart could do for him? Maybe killing me was the plan all along. Maybe he never wanted to save both of us. He tricked me into thinking we were brothers. He never loved me. He never liked me. He's been scheming with Dr. Willis this whole time.

Dr. Willis took Jeremiah Five, but at least Jeremiah Five loved me until the end. This Jeremiah never loved me. The worst part was that I wanted to help J7. I would have done anything for him. I wasn't afraid of Dr. Willis. She could sandwich me. She could scoop out my heart and give it away, but she couldn't *really* hurt me. Not like Jeremiah could hurt me. But I guess pigs never really get a choice—Dr. Willis taught me that. I thought maybe it was going to be different this time. Maybe I'd get to decide things myself. Apparently not. I was all alone in a house full of the people that I thought were my family.

Then I remembered. There was still someone that wanted to help me. Someone I knew deep in my perfect heart wanted me. If I could find Fairy Hogmother Saint Emily, she'd take care of me forever.

I waited until Justus went to the bathroom. I nosed the front door open, and I walked right out. I didn't say goodbye to anyone. I didn't turn back to look at the house. I just left.

I headed in the direction we went the first time Jeremiah wanted to get rid of me. I should have known back then that he didn't love me. If he did, he'd never try to get rid of me. He only forgave me when I saved him. And I wasn't even mad at him. I should have seen the signs, but I was too desperate for a new family. I wouldn't make that mistake again. The Rescue Ranch could be thousands of miles away. That would mean that it could take me up to thirty minutes to walk there. I would have to find a train or jetpack.

A school bus wouldn't help me. I'm already educated. I needed to wait for the ranch bus, but I had no idea where it stopped or how I'd get a bus pass. Then I saw my opportunity. A man and a little girl were loading a green van. The side door was wide open, and they were stuffing it with bags. Most vans aren't chatty. This one was.

It whispered, "Tropical Storm Delta is projected to make landfall in New Orleans on Saturday morning, but there is a chance it could change course. Some Houston residents are choosing to evacuate ahead of the storm, and some members of the Cajun Navy are already taking their airboats down to the Bayou City just in case Hurricane Harvey repeats itself. That's it for news on the nines. Next up is the best music of the eighties, nineties, and now, on…"

I stopped listening. They were afraid of Delta, but Delta wasn't even coming here. That means if someone borrowed their van it would be okay. As soon as the man and the little girl went back into the house, I knew what I had to do.

There's a movie where a handsome cop must save the president's daughter, but he has a problem. Everything he drives blows up after a few minutes. That's when he borrows a vehicle from a random lady. He promises to give it back, but it eventually gets exploded, too. *Commandeering* is when you borrow someone else's stuff because you need it more than they do. It was different than stealing because if you commandeer, it explodes afterward.

Once I got close, I noticed that the keys were in it. The van was running. It was like they wanted me to drive it. I struggled with the door and wiggled to the front. This van was not designed for pig borrowing, but I wedged myself between the two front seats. I stepped up to the console and used my nose to type in my destination. I tried typing *Rescue Ranch*, but it came out, H-H-I-N-Y-O.

Then the van said, "Harana Halli Karnataka, India, is your destination, directing to George Bush Intercontinental Airport." I was pretty sure that the van had the basic idea.

I was nervous. This was my first "felony." A *felony* is something that is against the rules but is okay if you really need to do it.

To go, I'd need to work the pedals and the wheel. Maybe even both at the same time. That's a little more complicated. The only problem is that I'm grown and don't fit down by the pedals. Beside the driver's seat there was an umbrella. I picked it up. It tasted terrible, and I took a minute to get it between the front two seats. I jabbed the pointy end at what I hoped was the bigger "GO!" pedal in the middle. While I was pressing on the pedal, my shoulder hit a stick and moved it. I dropped the umbrella to check what was going on outside. The houses slowly floated by. How could they do that? I thought I had to push the pedals for the car to move but apparently not.

I looked at the stick again. It was surrounded by letters. *P* for park. That's when you want to stop the car. *D* is for when you want to do a doughnut, and *N* is for when you want to take it nice and easy. I had moved the stick so it was now beside the *N*.

The van man ran out of the house. He yelled at me.

Sorry! I have to get to the Rescue Ranch, and I don't have my own car yet, I said. All he heard was "Oink."

He was gaining on me. This was my first "high-speed car chase." I tried to climb into the driver's seat so I wouldn't look suspicious.

I wished I had at least one hand. That would make this so much easier. The movie cop had two entire hands and a whole bunch of fingers, so it was easier for him to do the pedals and wheel. All I could really do was the horn, but I did it a lot. It didn't help. It was just loud and upsetting. I panicked because soon twelve police cruisers would be following me and shooting my tires. The van would explode.

Evasive maneuvers! I told the van because there was no button that said OUTRUN THE COPS. All the van heard was "Oink."

CHAPTER TWENTY-ONE

BOY

I needed to find J6. He's the only one that could help me with my plan. I couldn't tell my best friends what was going on. They'd snitch. Paloma worries too much, and Adnan always calls me out when he says I'm "doing something stupid." I guess that's because they're real friends.

I went into the living room and asked Justus where J6 went. She shrugged. Then I saw the front door wide open. Did I shut it on my way in or just kind of swat at it?

I poked my head out and heard a loud "Oink!"

J6 screamed somewhere up the street, but I couldn't see him.

He wasn't anywhere. I waited for the green van

inching its way across the road to move so I could see behind it. It eased forward slowly like it was just rolling down the gentle slope that ended in the bayou. It crossed into the wrong lane.

HONK! HONK! HONK!

Who was driving? I ran to the edge of my yard and saw through the windshield. A pig was driving that van toward my neighbor's house.

"OINK! OINK!" J6 screamed even though the van couldn't have been going any faster than five miles per hour. He panicked and honked the horn, and the wheel jerked to the side. The van turned toward my house.

It inched its way toward me and hit the curb. It rocked to a stop. J6 stumbled out. He was shaking like he'd just been in a real car crash.

"J6, get back inside the house."

He looked up the street and back at me.

"Don't run off. I almost have a plan. First, get your butt to our room," I said.

We ran inside while Jazmine ran outside to deal with the owner of the van.

We should have driven away together. Our house didn't feel like home. J6 was the only one who hadn't been lying to me for three months. The van might as well have crashed into this place. I couldn't live here. Dr.

Willis's betrayal was bad, but her whole job was to lie and kill. It infected my universe. Of course, my family didn't want J6 to have a name or get out of the crate.

When we got into my room and shut the door, I pushed my chair under the doorknob to keep Jazmine out. Then I dropped to a knee and hugged J6. He nuzzled his forehead into my shoulder.

I heard a door slam, then Jazmine's phone rang.

"It's Paloma," she announced.

I pushed the chair away and opened the door. She tossed her phone to me.

"Hi! I messaged you yesterday and I haven't heard back," said Paloma.

I had been too busy trying to figure out what to do about J6.

"I'm sorry."

"Are you still planning to go to the Dynamo game Friday?" she asked.

"Yeah. Why?"

J6 headbutted me and twitched his ears. I think he could hear what she was saying.

"I was wondering if you were being careful and evacuating," she said.

"No, the storm's not supposed to be bad. And there's no school."

"Yeah, you were right. We don't have school. I thought we had community service or something, like last year, but we don't. It's Staff Development Day on the calendar."

During the last community service day, Adnan sat next to me on the bus. He said if I didn't tell Paloma that I liked her, he would. I told her behind the cow shed at the farm. She smiled, but then disappeared.

I wanted to take her to the game, but I couldn't. I couldn't even tell her why she wouldn't get her jersey signed, or she'd tell my parents. I had to lie to Paloma. Disappoint her. J6 turned his head to the side and moved the tips of his ears every time I said anything. He was concentrating on me so hard I could barely think.

"I'm excited for the game, too. We're playing the LA Galaxy."

J6 rammed me with his head. Then he stared through my soul. His eyes looked like a person's eyes. They're brown like mine, but they're small compared to his big head. When they look at you, they can focus like a laser beam. I couldn't answer those eyes right now. I had to think and plan and lie, and I couldn't do that under his microscope. He stepped back and his head dropped so his nose was almost on the floor. For a minute, he looked the way I felt.

Paloma said, "Well, I want to go to the game with you. A lot. But I think you should cancel. Your heart device needs electricity, right?"

"Yeah."

"This storm might hit here and knock out the power. I googled it, and I think you should drive a little bit north just in case. I'll email you the flood maps. There are a bunch of motels outside of the flood area. It'd be like a vacation."

"Um."

Jazmine's phone beeped. The screen read ANNOYING BOY. That meant Adnan.

I told Paloma I'd call her back and hung up.

"I know Paloma is trying to tell you to skip out on the soccer game because she's afraid of a little rain, but if you don't go, I can't go," Adnan said. "See, that sounds like a bad plan. You can't let her trick you into depriving me of a celebrity experience—"

Jazmine's ID on her phone was right for once. Adnan was being an annoying boy.

"We're going Friday. Bye."

I hung up on him.

On Thursday, Dad insisted that J6 stay out of the crate all day. He fixed J6 oatmeal, burritos, and ice cream: a sort of last meal before execution. I tried to act normal, but that was like trying to breathe normally when a doctor tells you to. I always forget how.

Jazmine told Dad she caught J6 and me messing with the neighbor's van, but he felt too guilty to get us in trouble.

Justus was the only one I could trust. She sat on the floor in front of the TV watching the news broadcast about Tropical Storm Delta. We were supposed to get a little bit of rain, but Justus was terrified the storm would turn and come to Houston. J6 snuggled up to her. They showed pictures of people on roofs during Hurricane Katrina. She said if a hurricane came, she would hide in the attic.

"Don't worry about that, Justus. We'll be fine. If the storm was going to come by us, the doctors would evacuate me because of my LVAD. They didn't even cancel the game for tomorrow. Why are you watching this stuff anyway?" The remote was in front of J6. I changed it to PBS Kids.

I waved J6 toward my room.

CHAPTER TWENTY-TWO

PIG

Jeremiah confirmed that my family wanted to sandwich me. I thought Dr. Willis would pignap me and then keep me for most of the week. Jeremiah said she wanted to cut me open on Monday.

Monday is four days away, I said. Even though all he heard was "Oink," he understood.

Jeremiah made the face he always makes when he was trying to add fractions. He had no idea what to do. I didn't want to be a pulled-pork sandwich on an artisan bun with a large order of fries and a drink included. Worse, I still wasn't 100 percent sure my brother would want to help me, and I was too scared to listen to my pigheartedness.

Dad and Jazmine sometimes watch a TV show about listening to your heart. The host said the star of the show could give their heart to whoever they want. Actually, there were thirty people and the star had to pick one of them, but any pig would be lucky to get that much of a say in the matter. No one is supposed to steal your heart away.

Who was I now? I wasn't a therapy pig. Not even a sandwich. If I were a sandwich, at least there would be fries involved.

"I can't stay in this house anymore," Jeremiah said.

There was one thing I wanted if I couldn't get a brother.

I knocked the cards onto the floor and brought him, R-E-S-Q.

"What? Rest? What are you talking about?"

I went to Jeremiah's trash can and sniffed out a ranch packet. I licked it thoroughly, just to make sure it was clean, and I dropped it in front of him. I pointed at the letters on the floor again.

He finally understood. "Rescue Ranch. I know that place!"

I couldn't show him I was happy about it. I could barely move. How did he know about the land where pigs are the prime ministers, humans are butlers, and every breakfast comes without bacon? I cocked my head to the side. He opened his tablet.

The Rescue Ranch website showed men dangling dirty puppies above floodwater, a tiny emperor kissing a pig on the head, and a lot of grass. Best of all I saw her: Fairy Hogmother Saint Emily, founder, rescuer, hero. She was bottle-feeding a piglet in the picture.

"And I could visit you. It's less than an hour north of here."

Why would Jeremiah save me? Doesn't he want a new heart so he won't need his wires? I touched W-H-Y on the paper.

"They save animals from disasters and from labs. Do you want to go?"

What do *I* want? Jeremiah cared what I wanted because I mattered to him. Jeremiah would save me. No one ever saved a pig before.

Then I realized something. I backed up and blinked. How did I miss it? Jeremiah is pighearted, too.

He didn't want to harvest my organs, stick an apple in my mouth, and sandwich me. All he wanted was me, and I almost ran away from him.

I swear I'll never abandon you again, brother, I said. All he heard was, "Oink."

Then I pointed to the words and letters: JEREMIAH-H-E-A-R-T-?

"I'm fine. That's what this is for." He pointed to the

machine he wore near the waist of his pants. "Besides, without you there's other ways to get hearts. Leave it to me. We can both be okay. Will you go with me?"

I pointed to another word: YES.

It took him a little while to come back with Jazmine's phone, but finally he called them.

I listened to every word as he spoke, but he hung up looking disappointed.

"The Rescue Ranch can't take you now. They're getting ready for the storm. They said we should call back Wednesday. We need to get you somewhere people won't notice a pig. Like the woods, or underground, or in an abandoned building or something. Dr. Willis is supposed to get you Friday, so if we make it on our own for a day, I could get the Rescue Ranch to come save you. I have four batteries and each one lasts fourteen hours. I can be gone for sixty-six hours. That's almost three days."

That didn't seem right, but I was glad he was thinking it through.

"Where can we hide until I talk to them? Adnan wouldn't let me get away with something like this, and Paloma's parents would find out if I asked her to help."

Ugh. Her again. She eats pigs. If someone ate people, I wouldn't hang out with them. That's because I am a considerate brother. As soon as I heard her name I snorted and shook my head so hard my body moved with it.

"Wait, are you telling me something about Paloma?"

I snorted again, but Jeremiah didn't get it.

"The farm. The co-op farm I went to last year for our community service project. We could walk there from here. It's the perfect place to hide! You'll be safe."

I looked at him. I said, *Jeremiah, do you have any idea what happens to pigs at farms? Farms are even worse than room 23. Farms are basically piggy murder factories. It's like a million Palomas. How would you like it if I hid you at a serial killer's house?*

"They have tons of pigs. All we need to do is keep you safe tomorrow and tomorrow night. After that, the storm will be over. After that, we'll just call the Rescue Ranch and get them to adopt you and take me home."

I shook my head no.

Jeremiah sat down beside me. "I know you're scared, but trust me. I'd never let anything bad happen to you. I promise I'll keep you safe. I love you."

He'd never said that before. I didn't know what to say, so I just said, "Oink."

I was so excited I could barely sleep. I woke up before Jeremiah and picked out an outfit for him. Black cargo shorts and a black T-shirt were the sneakiest options. I tried to nudge him out of bed. He threw his arm at the alarm clock before it could scream the whole house awake. I snorted.

He checked his batteries and tucked the wires away.

He went to the bathroom. When he came back, he wrote his weight on a sheet of paper on his desk. He seemed a little worried about it. I took a look and didn't think gaining two pounds in a day was a big deal. It was all in his legs anyway. They were thick, but not nearly as thick as mine. Usually he only uses plastic wrap when he takes a shower, but this time he mummified himself in it before he put on his shirt. The storm wasn't going to hit us, but I still felt better knowing we were ready just in case.

He got dressed and packed a green backpack with snacks.

Why don't you bring your sleeping bag? Or some Band-Aids? I asked.

He nodded like he agreed with my oink. Then he took Justus's pink backpack out of the living room and stuffed it with three different kinds of hot chips. The shattering chips and crinkling bags made the loudest sound I'd ever heard. He stuffed every packet of ranch he could find in the front pocket. Then he undid the arms and used duct tape to extend them so I could wear it.

I'd thought about running away, but I never dreamed it would be like this. Yesterday, I thought I only had four days to live. I thought a pig like me would never get to decide what to do with himself. Now I was heading out on a new adventure with my brother. I wished Jeremiah Five was here to see us.

We snuck across the living room. Jeremiah stopped before opening the door. He looked down at me and I nodded at him. We didn't leave a note. We didn't leave a trace. We just left.

CHAPTER TWENTY-THREE

BOY

The lock clicked when our front door slammed shut. For the first time, this felt real. Dr. Willis said I needed to tell her if I gained weight really quickly. That meant that the right side of my heart wasn't pumping all the blood out of my veins and was starting to fail. This morning I noticed that I gained a little bit of weight and my legs felt swollen. I wanted to knock on Justus's window and beg her to let us back in, but J6 nosed my hand. His soft snout gave me some of his courage. It might have been boogers, but I'd like to imagine it was courage. We had to do this. No one was going to help us. The house slept but felt dangerous. It reminded me of the tangle of snakes Paloma and I found at the farm last year.

The co-op farm was probably no more than two miles away, but it might take a while to find. I remembered two ladies and a bunch of pigs, but mostly I remembered how my heart felt when I told Paloma how I felt. It seemed like it was working just fine then. I knew for sure there were plenty of places to hide because after she ran off, I couldn't find her.

J6 and I could make it to the farm this morning, but I didn't have Jazmine's phone to get directions. Also, that meant I'd have to find another way to get back in touch with the Rescue Ranch. But if I did have it, she'd use it to track me down.

We passed the house where retired people lived with their retired rooster that crowed so loudly, I could hear it from home. From the sidewalk in front of the rooster house, the gap in the buildings let me see downtown skyscrapers. I lived in the country and the city at the same time.

After two blocks, it started to rain. I needed a break. I think I felt worse than I did when J6 and I went to the Oasis Market. Once I saved him, I actually might want to talk to Dr. Willis. It took me a long time to catch my breath. That wasn't good. The LVAD helped the left part of my heart pump the blood through my body, but the right part of my heart was on its own. It needed to pump blood through my lungs, and it had to keep up with a machine. It wasn't doing great.

I sat on the curb with my feet in the street and got the butt of my jeans wet. I was going to take better care of myself.

A light blue car slowed down, and I tried to wish it away. I scooted back onto the sidewalk and turned my head. I imagined the doors would open and the driver would take me, or she'd call the cops. The pictures grew so huge in my head that I hated her by the time she rolled her window down.

"Are you all right? Do you need help?"

How old did she think I was?

I slowed my breathing. "I'm fine."

I watched her hands to see if she would jump out of the car or grab for her phone, but she didn't. She left. The key to taking a pig through Houston is to look like you know what you're doing. I didn't realize I had my hand on J6's back to soak up more bravery.

We had to stop one more time because I was having a hard time getting enough air. I was afraid I'd end up passing out on the side of the road before we even got to the farm. J6 raised his eyebrows. His tail stopped shaking. He was worried. He nosed me. We kept going.

Finally, we got to the Urban Organic Co-Op. J6's

ears perked up. He shifted his weight from one back foot to another and his tail made figure eights. He'd seen the other pigs through the fence. I froze.

"Oink!"

I grabbed his backpack and yanked him around a corner.

"Shh, stay still." I peeked at a school bus pulling up. Community service day always starts early so we can work outside before it gets too hot. J6's life depended on hiding for at least a day. If any of those sixty kids turned us in, he'd die. I waited until the bus stopped and kids started going inside. We walked along the fence surrounding the farm until I found a back gate. A gray cat that was in worse shape than Justus's stuffed bear sat just inside. I climbed over and let J6 in behind me. He hid behind the cow's stall. I caught my breath before I scouted out the pigpen and tried to avoid the group of kids filing through the other gate. I thought I was a ninja until I heard a familiar voice.

"Hey! Look at that little boy!"

I looked up. Most of the kids dodging puddles on the way to the barn were too busy to pay attention. The only one looking in my direction had pink curls poking out of her hood. Monica.

"Wait for me, J6," I said.

I hid my face and caught up to the group in the barn before a teacher noticed. Even if Monica wouldn't turn me in, I didn't want anything to do with her. She was the worst.

I huddled alongside sixty kids in rain jackets. Any of them could notice that I didn't belong, but I was too distracted to care. A woman who looked like she was wearing a Little Mermaid wig waited for us to get quiet.

"Hi everyone. Welcome to the co-op. My wife and I don't run this alone. Lots of people in the community take turns working here. Then the food we get goes to the shelters in the community. The storm that was supposed to hit New Orleans is turning toward us now, and this area usually floods. There isn't an evacuation order or anything, so don't worry about that. It's only supposed to be a tropical storm, but we live here, we work here, and we'll lose everything if we get much rain. That's where you come in."

Monica called out, "How much will you pay us?"

The teacher shushed her. Monica put on headphones.

"Divide up into two groups," said the woman.

Three girls in front of me immediately locked arms like red rover. A tall kid beside me looked in my direction, and I felt bad for walking away from him.

"One group needs to box up hay and animal feed; the other group needs to work on packing up our supplies."

It took about three minutes of negotiation for the kids to divide. I tried to avoid getting spotted so I wandered through groups on my way to the open barn door.

"If it's going to be so bad, why don't we have to evacuate?"

"This whole thing is fake news."

"I shouldn't have worn these kicks."

"I'm going to my tia's house tonight. Just in case."

"This is gross."

"Hey! That pig's out!"

My group spilled out the door and flowed toward J6. He should have been hiding. This was bad.

"I think I can catch it."

"I'll tackle it."

"Don't call her an it."

Monica shoved her way to the front. "It's a girl. You don't hit girls. Ever. Leave her alone. Look at her backpack. It's pink."

J6 shook his head no. Monica knelt down to try and pet him, but her phone fell out of her hoodie pocket, came unplugged from her headphones, and started blasting something that sounded like Demi Lovato. I'd never heard the song. Adnan's job is to play new songs for me. Then he tells me all about the drama the artists are going through because "it's important to keep up with current events."

J6 backed away, but then he tilted his head to the side and perked his ears up. He looked at the circle surrounding him. I knew he never should have watched *Step Up*.

I stared at him and tried to tell him *Please don't, please don't, please don't* with my mind. He was on the run. If he got caught by Gen-e-heart or my family, he would get killed. His nose twitched to the beat. He should hide. But he was thirsty for attention. He also had a dancing addiction and too much confidence. His tail started swaying. Then the feet picked it up. Once I saw his butt get moving, I knew there was no stopping him. He always thought he could dance his way out of his problems. Ten kids whipped out phones. J6 looked nervous but kept dancing.

Then the song changed to Ariana Grande. J6 froze. He shook his head. Monica skipped the song. J6 shook his head no again. It was the only time in recorded history that kids on a field trip silently paid attention to something. She settled on her last choice. An old Bruno Mars song. J6 nodded. Then he kept moving his head and started dancing again.

"Did the pig just pick the song?"

"Whoa!"

He stuck his snout in the dirt and drew a smiley face. The kids backed up. Now he was really feeling himself and kept writing. 😊-I-N-K-I

He pointed at it and oinked. Every kid but me applauded. They kept filming him. This was a disaster. We were supposed to be hiding.

"I'm going to go show the lady!" One kid ran off, then a bunch more followed. I could already see the teacher tearing over to disperse the mob. J6 panicked, rolled around on his writing—smooshing the snacks I packed—and dashed through the kid herd. I followed the devastation until I found him.

"Over here! J6!" He ran to me and I brought him behind a haystack. I guided him to the pig pen and let him in. I ripped the duct tape off Justus's backpack and threw it into the hog house. J6 leapt into a mud puddle and wallowed until he was covered in filth. Now he could blend in. I climbed out and backed away from him until I bumped into someone.

"Sorry." I looked up into a mess of faded pink curls.

"Watch it. Wait, you don't go to my school. Aren't you that little boy from the soccer game?"

Suddenly, phone alerts rippled across the farm.

"Wait, are you this Amber Alert? Are you okay? It

says you need a doctor? Did someone take you? Did you run away from someone? Was someone hurting you?" She glanced down at her phone and read the rest of the message. I leapt into the pig pen. I scrambled over to the only place I could find cover. I crawled into the hog house. I heard yelling.

"Hey, miss! Miss! I found the little boy from the Amber Alert! I found him. He was with the dancing pig that got out. We need to help him."

I obliterated every rule Dr. Willis gave me, but I was too tired to care. Too tired to see if anyone believed that girl. Too tired to keep my eyes open.

CHAPTER TWENTY-FOUR

PIG

Jeremiah climbed into the pig condominium with my backpack. He was hiding from the Pink-Haired Music Girl, but she was busy yelling at Tall Lady. She kept pointing at the pen. Tall Lady quietly talked to her and made a Butler Jazmine face. The yelling was not working. I watched them until Pink-Haired DJ gave up and huffed away to pout in the barn.

The condo was haunted by a ghost cat no one else could see. He sat on the roof and judged me. I inspected my accommodations. There was no grass, only mud. At first, it looked like a wreck, but I splashed around a little more. Then I rolled over and let myself sink. This wasn't regular mud. It was very expensive luxury mud like at the spa. Spas are places where you pay a million dollars to get luxury mud put on your face, but these pigs were so luxurious that they wore mud all over. I stood back up and the fancy pigs stared at me...like they knew me...like I was their king.

I surveyed my subjects. These pigs were almost as beautiful as I was, but they had huge yellow earrings. They had the style and swag I would expect from my people. The only black spotted pig danced over to me and snuffled my neck. A bold move. He didn't need to tell me his name. I knew it as soon as I saw him: Vice President Kevin Bacon. Jeremiah was hiding in the condo. He was safe for the time being, so I made my first proclamation.

I, your king, have arrived! I will rule you with humility. You may call me King, Your Royal Highness, King Jeremiah the Sixth, or Most Exalted One. You are all my subjects. Now, I rest. That's what I meant to say. Instead I said, "Oink. Snort. Oink. Ooooink."

Only the ghost cat and Vice President Kevin Bacon seemed to understand.

I hung out with Jeremiah in the pig condo until the rain picked up and the bus ate the children. Jeremiah fell asleep and some fire-headed lady screamed that it was time to eat.

She threw oats at us. I oinked at her to explain that I take my oats in oatmeal form with a dash of nutmeg and one spoon of brown sugar, preferably in a nonslip bowl. I'm not some kind of animal.

After I was finished with my order, I turned around to see that all the oats were gone, and I'd missed out on lunch. That's when I heard the truck pull up. I couldn't read what was written on the side, but the truck was probably for some kind of pig awards show. Only the most attractive pigs like Babe and Ms. Piggy get to go. That's why we got spa mud. We were preparing. I'd get to go on TV and serve as a "strong role model" for delinquent pigs. Jeremiah and Vice President Kevin Bacon could be my unappreciated assistants, and I could throw phones at them. They'd like that. I mentally prepared myself for the diva life. But first, Red was going to give me my makeover.

A makeover is when people decide you have a lot of inner beauty and outer ugly, so they try to help. They inform you that the way you look is wrong and make you look good enough to walk around in society without having a bag over your head. I would have been offended about the idea, but I had luxury puddle snot all over me. I graciously accepted the offer, and Red led me behind a wall.

I got close enough to see the words on the side of the truck: ANDERSON'S MEATS.

RUN, VICE PRESIDENT KEVIN BACON! These people are killers! They are going to sandwich us! Run for your lives. That's a meat truck! The pigs heard "Oink, oink."

The red traitor led me to a hose and scrub brush behind a wooden wall. She stuck my head in a rope loop.

"How'd you get so filthy? I can't have you messing up that nice truck," she said.

She scrubbed my ears and gasped. She leaned close to admire my tattoo, and a second later she jumped up. Maybe she thought I was too tough to sandwich. She left me tied to the wall and sprinted away. I wiggled free and undid the latch with my nose.

Come on, Vice President Kevin Bacon, we got to get out of here. He oinked at me and stayed in the pen. He'd never abandon his constituents.

I dove into a pile of hay. It looked prickly, but it was surprisingly soft. The other woman led the pigs one by one onto the truck. Jeremiah was sleeping, but he'd be safe for now.

I could hear Red talking. "The one I was washing ran off. I noticed a tattoo on his ear, so I went to find you. I don't think he's ours, but we need to find him anyway.

We need to get him out of here before the storm gets any worse."

"Did you call the Rescue Ranch again? Can they accommodate everyone until the hurricane's over?"

"Yeah, I double checked. We'll load the pigs first. Don't worry, honey, I won't let anything happen to them. But we need to leave soon. Hurricane Delta might hit category two and it's heading right for us."

The Anderson Meats truck is either a big trick, or they're trying to save all the pigs and just borrowing the truck. Jeremiah would be fine for now, but I needed to get aboard. This is what Jeremiah wanted. I was finally going to be free. Either way, I'd never ever have to go back to room 23. He'd be happy for me. I wished I could say goodbye. But I couldn't. I took off running toward the gate.

The ducks quacked their approval.

A horse tried to high-five me.

A goose almost bit me because all geese are murderous psychopaths. The gate was open.

Just before I placed one happy little hoof into the land of liberty, I saw the ghost cat. Cats have a language all their own, and when they're alone they sing, do flips, teleport, and shoot lightning bolts. I saw a documentary about that.

So, you're just going to leave Jeremiah alone? They said this hurricane is "cat. two," so that's two cats of trouble. That's basically three sharknados, and you're going to let that happen to your own brother? Just like you let them take Jeremiah Five? What if he gets wet in the storm? I thought you were a health care professional, tutor, and handsome role model. I guess not. At least I think that's what the cat meant to say. All I heard was "Meow."

But you don't understand. I need to get to safety. If I stay with Jeremiah, I might not be able to run away again. If I don't run away, I'll go back to room 23, I said, but all the cat heard was "Oink."

He looked me dead in the eyes and meowed again. He meant to say, *That's why people eat you instead of cats. You have no heart.*

I have an excellent heart with strong ventricle walls, and that's my problem, I oinked.

I finally got a chance to decide what to do with myself, and I couldn't. I closed my eyes and listened to my pigheartedness. I could hear it again even though the fear was a little louder. It said: *brother.*

I turned around. With my head hanging low, I walked back past the murder-goose. I almost got my tail bitten off. I walked through the cow's still-open gate and looked up into its beautifully mascaraed eyelashes.

I crawled into the pig condo and found Jeremiah on his back in the corner. Suddenly, I didn't mind missing my ride. I watched the other animals get loaded onto the truck. I wondered if those animals would eventually get eaten.

I never ate any living thing. Even before we were brothers, Jeremiah used to feed me bites of his food. Sometimes I'd get a bite of hamburger (it isn't really ham, that's just the name), chicken fingers (chickens don't have fingers), or fish sticks (which are mostly stick). Jeremiah wouldn't eat when his family would have schnitzel or carnitas. He'd pick at the sides and ignore the pig parts of it. Out of respect. That's what a good buddy does. A good buddy doesn't eat your relatives in front of you. For example, I wouldn't eat Butler Jazmine, no matter how good she smelled.

Now Jeremiah doesn't eat any meat at all: no cows or chickens or even squirrels. He's changed a lot since I've known him. I snuggled up to his side and kept him warm while the rain picked up. I tried to stay awake for our last afternoon together. After I took him home, I would need to run away for real. But I fell asleep.

CHAPTER TWENTY-FIVE

BOY

My head slipped off the backpack I was using as a pillow and ended up in a puddle. I rolled over and pressed my mouth shut under the water, but I could taste the slime. Before I opened my eyes, I imagined the sludge came to life and attacked my face with a slippery tentacle. It oozed into my ear, filled my skull, and lapped at my brain. It was too dark to see the pig licking my cheek.

My new bed was an icy puddle, but the sound of rain slamming against a metal roof was almost enough to make me want to go back to sleep. Only my stomach was warm. J6 must have slept beside me to keep me from freezing. I smiled. J6 marched outside.

A few months ago, I was terrified of Adnan visiting.

I thought going outside might kill me. Wallowing in a literal pigsty wasn't on the list Dr. Willis sent home from the hospital. All I could see was the faint outline of J6 and a gray spot that must be the opening to the hog house. I splashed to the door after my brother.

I stuck my head out and turtled it right back in. The rain hurt like it was solid. J6 stood by the door, and I used him to help me push myself up. The wind almost knocked me down. It was hard, but I stood up and stretched. I expected to feel better, but my back and neck exploded in pain.

What time was it? The sky was completely black. Zero percent battery, powered-down black. At least the streetlights were still lit. I had to squint to keep the rain out of my eyes. The pigs were gone. All of the animals were gone. The only sound was rain. I listened again and it wasn't so relaxing. It was like a machine gun in a movie. Maybe all the animals washed away. Even the ground seemed like it got packed up and shipped off.

Rain. Washed away. Puddle. I panicked. I felt my stomach. The plastic wrap was still there. I felt under my hoodie. The unit controller was still dry. I poked my head into my shirt. The battery lights were still green. I left around five a.m. That meant these two batteries would last twenty-eight hours. As long as I changed them before tomorrow, I'd be fine. We were both okay.

I'd never been this cold, wet, or dirty. I couldn't stand up and had no idea what I'd do. The storm was getting worse. Today I gave up a soccer game, a signed jersey, and a warm bed, but I saved J6.

I had no idea what time it was, but it had to be at least midnight. I'd never been out at this time before. The farm was empty, but my heart was full. The sky was dark, but I felt bright and sunny.

I pulled my hoodie tighter. The whole time I'd been standing here I hadn't seen any cars drive by. The cows' barn might be empty. Maybe we could hide in there for a few hours? Then, once the rain stopped, I'd find somewhere to clean up. Maybe the rain would help?

"We'll hide in the barn until morning. Then we'll try to call the Rescue Ranch again."

"Oink." He shook his head no.

"We'll need to get to a phone."

I felt like a backpack of junk food snacks might not have been all we needed.

"Oink!"

I shooed him away. A second later, my knees buckled. He'd knocked me down. Once I was on his level, he looked me in the eye and said, "Oink. Oink."

"Do you want to go home?"

He cocked his head sideways again. I yelled, "HOME?"

He nodded.

"No. CALL THE RANCH. THEN GO HOME."

I'd go home without him. I left that part off.

He headbutted me.

I raced toward the door of the house the farmers lived in. I pulled open the storm door and pounded on the red door underneath. No answer. I rang the doorbell. Nothing. I peeked in the side windows and all the lights were off. Finally, I tried to open the front door. I was relieved when I realized it was locked. I didn't actually want to break into anyone's house. We didn't have any better options. We'd have to go home.

I crawled back into the hog house and got Justus's backpack and put it back on J6. Maybe I could explain everything to Mom and Dad. Maybe they'd understand.

I went into the back corner of the barn and put the unit controller and batteries in the shower bag. They should be okay as long as they didn't get dunked in water. I should be okay as long as nothing hit my driveline. Talking on the phone in the rain is different than dropping it in the toilet.

On the way home, the rain went from falling hard to

switching directions every few seconds like a car wash. It knocked me down, and I brought my elbows under me just in time. I would rather break my arms than yank the driveline loose. From the ground, I noticed a red SUV rocking on its tires. I wrapped my arms around J6's neck, and he helped pull me up. His shoulders came up to my hip bone, and I could rest some of my weight on him without having to lean over. He could support me. I kept my hand on him while we made it down the street.

The streams running down the sides of the road swelled into rivers that filled my sneakers. I thought I was dripping from the water, but maybe my legs were sweating. Dr. Willis warned me about that. Sweaty legs were another sign of heart failure. We stopped five times, but I couldn't sit. Even the sidewalk was disappearing under rushing water. For a minute, I wondered if we could make it back, but J6 remembered the way home. I wanted to stop, but he towed me back to my street.

After we got within a few houses, a loud crack exploded behind us and everything went dark. J6 stopped. If my heart still beat, it would have stopped, too. I needed that electricity. I needed to recharge. I knelt beside him, and he nuzzled into my side. Then he pointed his snout at the ground, and I held on to the backpack.

I sat. I wasn't going anywhere. I couldn't see. I wasn't even sure what direction we came from. I held on to J6, and he started moving again. I pulled back on him and tried to stop him, but he wouldn't slow down. I had to keep up. After a few minutes, he turned and we squished through some grass. A flashlight beam from inside shot out of a house I recognized. I was home. I was relieved until it hit me: I didn't tell anyone where I was going. Maybe they thought I was dead. When they found out I was alive, they'd kill me. The door seemed too dangerous to knock on, so J6 dodged around me and head-butted it.

The storm door swung open, the wind caught it, and slammed against the side of the house hard enough to crack the glass. The front door opened to swallow me, and an arm reached out like a tongue and yanked me in.

The living room had never been warmer.

Jazmine hugged me so hard she actually picked me up, before throwing me down.

"You're disgusting. Change."

"Where are Mom and Dad? What time is it?"

Jazmine turned away from me. She held a huge flashlight. I pushed into the house.

"It's ten fifty. At night."

"Mom? Dad?"

"Take off those shoes."

I kicked them off in the kitchen. I was heading for my parents' room when Jazmine caught up to me. She shoved me toward the bathroom and shut the door. A minute later, the door swung open and something flew inside. Then she handed me the flashlight. I looked around. Fresh clothes, and two towels.

"Where are Mom and Dad?" I shouted. I realized I hadn't seen Justus yet, either.

"You're freezing. Clean up and put the new pants on. No shirt. Let me change your dressings. Now."

I didn't think I needed to, but when I picked up the flashlight, my hand was shivering so hard it strobed around the room like the lights at a school dance. I changed and got dressed. I left my wet clothes in the hamper. As soon as I opened the door, I found Jazmine in the kitchen, sponging off J6 with her right hand. Her left hand held her cell phone up to her ear. Justus sat on the kitchen counter. Her feet were in the sink.

Jazmine talked to me without looking, "We went to the cops. Filed a missing person's report. Amber Alert.

Mom called all of the hospitals. Then she called the morgues. Sit down."

Jazmine dialed a number, and J6 got away from her.

"Where are they?" I asked.

She stared at her phone. She wouldn't answer me. Something was wrong.

I raced into the living room, and Jazmine threw her phone onto the couch and cussed.

"Cell towers are out. They should have been back by now."

She sat down and shook her head while she cut the plastic wrap off me.

"You're so lucky. You know that. How could you..." She kept shaking her head. My bandages were pretty dry, but she replaced them and put antibiotic cream around the driveline hole. She wrapped me back up. She switched out my batteries.

She went into my room and threw a long-sleeve shirt and hoodie at me.

"I'm going to find them."

"What? Find them? Find them where?"

She pulled me across the room and whispered, "About two hours ago they issued an emergency evacuation. An ambulance came to our door because they didn't know you were missing. People with airboats are out looking for you right now."

"Airboats?"

"The ones with the big fans on the back. Anyway, Mom and Dad went looking for you on foot. They probably won't come home without you, so I'm going to get them."

"No, um, let me. I can go. I started all of this. I need to go. Let me."

"Aahhh," she quietly growl-screamed at me. "Do you have any idea... I'm just disgusted with how... how could you?"

She was shaking. I looked down and squirmed before I realized I was copying what J6 would do. I stood up straight and looked her in the eye.

"Come here." She put hands on both of my shoulders. "I'm glad you're safe. You shouldn't have left, but you can't fix this."

I yanked free. "I ran off and they left. This is on me. I need to find them."

"No. You're not being a hero; you're being selfish. This is your fault, but I'm going because I know what streets they were checking. Just six inches of water can knock you off your feet. I can swim. I don't need batteries. I don't need to stay dry. I know first aid. I can be back in thirty minutes. They're not far. You might have even passed them while you were taking your time getting back here. Just watch Justus."

She put on her coat, threw open the door, and stepped into the storm.

CHAPTER TWENTY-SIX

PIG

It made sense that Butler Jazmine would leave me in charge of these kids. I dragged Jeremiah's lazy butt home. The president should have given me a Teen Choice Award for heroism.

Still, as soon as she left, I felt very much unsupervised. Justus cried louder than the wind outside. It sounded like Jeremiah One teamed up with some dinosaurs and they were trying to break in.

And we had a "blackout." That means everyone who has hands gets flashlights. Those of us who do not have hands have to sit in the dark. We can't even watch TV, even though we had recorded three movies starring the

Rock. He was the actor who will play me in the R-rated action musical about my life.

Jeremiah got so bored without Dwayne Johnson that he yanked on a string in the ceiling and ripped a square hole in it. A ladder fell down, and he climbed up it and into the house's skull. He threw a cooler down and opened the freezer to fill it with ice.

Ice is cold, unflavored toilet juice. It doesn't even deserve to be called water, but he put the ice cream in there, too, so it was all right. Ice cream is the smartest thing science ever invented. I tried to get up the ladder to see what else was up there, but ladders discriminate because only people with hands can use them.

Jeremiah filled up a bunch of containers with water because he thought we would run out. I told him there was plenty of water outside. The toilet served up all you can drink. He wasn't listening. While Jeremiah got more water, Queen Justus camped out on the kitchen counter because she thought the house would flood. Jeremiah and Justus couldn't seem to agree if there was too much water or not enough.

Jeremiah seemed like he was about to collapse before we got in, but now he zoomed around the house doing everything he could. It was probably his new batteries that gave him the boost.

"I'll guard the queen," I volunteered. I'm pretty sure the fuzzy-headed palace guards in England don't oink. I marched back and forth across the kitchen. I'd focus and never get distracted from my duties unless I found a cookie under the edge of the cabinet or smelled a chip under the fridge.

The queen surprised me when I heard the cupboards slam shut. She stood on the counter.

That seems dangerous— I said. When she heard my oink, she spun around and nearly fell. Without thinking I ran to her. I should have been smart. She could have squished me, but my legs know the queen's safety comes first. She caught herself and climbed down. She had a whole bag of cookies in her hand.

She moved her eyebrows up and down.

"Daddy's secret stash."

I'd never admired her more.

We sat on the floor and she split them up—one for me, one for her.

Jeremiah was a lot more work, but Queen Justus was my sister, too. That technically made me a king or a prince, at least a prime minister, but I already could have guessed that. I looked up at her and shivered. She cuddled with me and grabbed my head. She scratched my ear. Part of being the queen's guard is pretending to be afraid so the queen can be brave.

"Oink," I said.

"Oink," she said.

"Justus, where are you?"

"In here!" she yelled.

Since Jazmine was gone, Jeremiah was trying to be the new butler of the house. The butler is a servant, but also in charge. He was bossy, but he brought us entertainment. He interrupted our cuddle time by tossing a blanket at her. He handed her his tablet. He told her she could play a game with headphones on, then he marched off to make himself feel helpful.

"You're the boss, Jerry." She laughed and I snorted. We both knew she was the queen, but since she's royalty she knew it was not nice to rub people's faces in it. She gave me the rest of the cookies I deserved and sat on the couch. I hoped she wasn't afraid anymore. I followed Jeremiah into the bathroom. He turned on the faucets in the tub.

This is no time for a bath, Jeremiah. Honestly, I said. He ignored me.

The queen needed me more than Jeremiah did. She definitely needed me more than she needed his tablet.

Your Majesty? I called down the hall.

She didn't oink back.

I waited. Jeremiah wanted me right here, so here was where I'd stay. The water inched up the side of the tub, and it reminded me of the streets filling up. It made sense that Queen Justus was scared.

I hope Justus is doing okay. I might go check on her, I said. All Jeremiah heard was "Oink," but that didn't matter. The front door slammed open. Someone screamed and ran. I raced out of the bathroom, past the hall with its big ladder, and into the living room.

I started out the door. Where was the queen? I checked the couch where I saw her last. Nope. Not in her room. Or the bathroom. Or Butler Jazmine's room, or Mom and Dad's room.

Justus was gone.

CHAPTER TWENTY-SEVEN

BOY

JG scampered down the hall after we heard the crash. He should've been back by now. Mom, Dad, and Jazmine were gone, too. Everything hurt inside and out, and I deserved it. I wanted to lie down and stop the pictures that sped through my brain. This was all my fault, and I couldn't even tell anyone.

The rain hit the house in sheets, like the drops schemed in the clouds and attacked together. It sounded like the waves at Galveston. They were out there trying to find someone who lied to them. I wanted to pray, but I couldn't think of the right words. I usually only prayed at church or when I lost my tablet. I dried my hands and stuck my head out the door.

"J6? Justus?" I called out.

The front door gaped open like J6's mouth before he chomps on your arm. My first thought was to run outside and look for them, but I noticed the ladder to the attic was still down. I shut the front door and climbed up. It took a minute for my eyes to adjust. Justus was there, sitting with her back to the roof. The spiderwebs around her made it look like they caught her. She didn't care. It might as well be a blanket fort. The tablet lit her serious little face. Professor Fuzzy Shark and Mr. Stinky Bear cuddled in her lap.

"Jerry!"

"Why's the front door open?"

"I opened the front door to see if Mom and Dad were there. The wind was really loud, and I decided that it would be better to wait it out up here."

"Why?"

She rolled her eyes. "Didn't you see the videos of the people on their roof from the other hurricane? When the hurricane comes, the streets all flood and then sometimes the houses fill up. That's when you need to go on the roof so the boats can rescue you. Those boats are already on the way, so I'm just waiting up here."

J6 was out there by himself. He must have taken off looking for Justus. Because of me. Now I had to find him. Justus would be okay. She's smarter than I am. Besides, it didn't matter if I got lost. Everyone would be better off without me.

"If the house fills up, won't you be stuck up here? You can't go through the roof."

Justus thought about it and shrugged. I honestly didn't have any other suggestions. Ideally, her parents would be here to tell her what to do. Ideally, she'd have a better brother. At least I could tell her the truth.

"J6 got out—"

"How could you let that happen? He was with you. I was watching him, and you took him because you think you're responsible even though you ran away. You think you're the boss, but you're not."

"I'm going to get him. You—"

"You're running away. Again? I'm eight. You're just leaving me here? I am not allowed to be left alone by myself."

"You need to stay here and make sure the storm doesn't get you."

"Obviously."

"Take off your headphones so you can hear when everyone gets home."

"Duh."

I climbed back down from the attic and found

windbreaker pants and a raincoat. I put my controller and batteries into the shower bag and put all of that in a baggie. I duct-taped around where the driveline connected. I used the tape to make a handle and slung it over my shoulder. Then I wrapped a roll of plastic wrap around my stomach. I taped it around the edges. I put on the raincoat and tucked it into the windbreaker pants. I taped around my ankles, my stomach, my arms, and my neck. Finally, I taped over the zipper. I felt waterproof. It took five minutes, but I hesitated before I ran outside.

I wrote a note on the kitchen notepad.

Justus safely in attic, and the tablet is mostly charged. J6 escaped. Going to get him. I paused a few seconds and realized it wouldn't be enough. Mom might worry. I added, *Will wear jacket and plastic wrap. I'll watch for traffic. Love, Jeremiah. PS I'm back from running away. Also, sorry.*

This time, I wouldn't sprint. If I did, it would be just like the soccer game. If I exerted myself and got lucky, I'd end up in the hospital and not floating down the bayou. This time, I'd be smart.

It was all up to me. I stepped into the hurricane. My body was more exhausted than I could remember, but I could make it for just long enough to find J6, get home, and figure out a way to save him. I had to.

CHAPTER TWENTY-EIGHT

PIG

What if she was hiding near the house?

I waited. I didn't lie down, but I went to every house near ours and looked into the backyard. It took a while, but after I was sure she wasn't around there, I inched my way down the street. The wind almost knocked me over. Can pigs actually fly? I'd find out soon. I felt the edge of the sidewalk and tried to walk down the gutter so I didn't get confused, but the water almost went up my snout. I almost got hit by something bouncing down the street like a giant soccer ball.

Where did she go? I tried to look into the wind, but it was all dark. The rain made it impossible to smell her. Then I realized Justus is a tiny fairy queen, and the wind doesn't respect royalty. She might have been the thing bouncing down the street!

I ran with the wind on my tail.

CRASH, CRASH, CRASH!

I backflipped to safety. I had no idea what was chasing after me, but I'm pretty sure it was Megatron.

Justus! Your Majesty, where are you! I focused and tried hard to make words this time. I moved my mouth the way people do. All that came out was "Oink," but she'd still know me anywhere. At least I'm close to the ground, and I have short strong legs. After I find her, she can grab onto me and I can help her home. I realized I was going toward the park where we went to the festival. I shuddered. The street lit up for a minute and got dark again. My strong heart with excellent ventricular formation beat harder when I got to the next street. Some lights across the way worked, but it seemed like the road was moving. And splashing. Three cars sank into it. The whole street was underwater.

I turned around. I thought this was the street beside the park, but it didn't look like a street.

What if Justus got blown away, then splashed into this mess?

What if I got swept away? Can pigs swim?

When I got into the water, I knew I was braver than

I thought. When I took a few steps, I realized I was stronger than I thought. When I tripped off the sidewalk, fell into the deeper water on the street, and the flood swept under my hooves so fast that I flipped over, I realized I was stupider than I thought. I guess I really did have a human brain.

I tried to breathe, but water filled my mouth. I coughed, and kicked, and flipped back over. Almost as much water filled the air.

Help! I screamed, but all I heard was the rain. This time I could barely hear my own oink. The wind kidnapped it. Just like it kidnapped my sister. It couldn't get any worse.

CHAPTER TWENTY-NINE

BOY

It only took a second for me to catch him with my flashlight. Then I almost tripped. I pointed the flashlight back at the ground. Walking felt like trying to stand on top of a car doing seventy-five miles per hour in the rain. Wearing roller skates. I had to bend my knees and keep my head down.

This wind was stealing the air out of my lungs. I stopped and tried to force oxygen back into my body, but what I saw nearly knocked the breath out of me again.

Houston is mostly concrete. All the rain drains into the bayous because there's not much dirt to soak it up. If this kept going, the water would make it up my street. I felt like that cold dirty water filled my heart. What could I do now?

"J!" My whole soul left when I screamed that. I had to suck my spirit back in. "SIX!"

I could barely see in front of me. The raindrops lit up, but everything else blurred.

Cars in the middle of the road filled with water. I couldn't see whether or not there were people trapped inside. Then I saw him. J6 spun in the current like a pink balloon in the wind... and I had let go of the string. This could be the last time I'd ever see him.

"J6!"

Please see me, I prayed. *Please God, help him. Someone help. Anyone.* I looked around for an ambulance or a lifeguard. I begged the eye of the hurricane to look down on me.

The convenience store was still mostly dry. The flooding filled the street, but was only a few inches deep on the sidewalk. The current floated J6 across the street. The park was much lower than the street and the water would be over my head, but I wouldn't go out that far.

I stepped onto the sidewalk and felt solid. I sloshed after J6 for a block as I tried to keep him in the beam of my flashlight, but my legs got heavier. J6 shrank and dimmed. I felt like I just finished a marathon. I couldn't stop now. Everything would be all right as long as I didn't go any deeper. As long as I stayed off the curb.

I walked with the current. The wind picked up and J6 squealed. I tried to run. I held the shower bag under my arm and reminded myself that as long as the water stayed below the driveline hole, below my belly button, I was safe. The curb couldn't be that high. It wasn't that much water. The most it could be was a foot. I could take a step to my right, or I could lose my brother.

I thought I'd keep my feet under me. Instead, as soon as the water slipped over my ankles, the wind picked up. When I tried to set my other foot in the deep, my sneaker slipped. I belly-flopped and thrashed back toward the curb. The water ripped me away from the sidewalk and dragged me toward the area that used to be an esplanade. It wasn't deep. I could touch the pavement, but it was so fast and overwhelming I couldn't stop myself. It felt like I was sliding down the side of a mountain. My head went under. The water tasted the way garbage smelled. It filled my mouth. I didn't let go of the flashlight. My head smashed into a metal bar. I snatched at the bar with my free hand. My fingers slipped away. I kicked and forced my head up.

I got the flashlight back out of the water and saw J6 again. His leg was caught on the upper bill of the pelican sculpture. This was my chance. I kicked my foot out, but this time it didn't hit the road. I couldn't see where I was, but I must have been washed off the street. Now I was just keeping afloat over the park. My brain told my free arm to paddle. Instead, it shook.

I felt like an astronaut with a hole in his suit. I kicked my heavy feet and felt the tape around my stomach slip. I panicked and flailed and felt water splash through the neck hole. Each breath out, a scream. I coughed. I kicked. The water spun. The flashlight's beam waved through the air. J6 swirled around. Kick. Breathe. Kick. Reach. Breathe. Breathe. I stretched my arm. Fingertips felt a string. No. A tail. Breathe in. Kick. Kick. I hugged something warm and angry, but it was the only thing left in a dark world.

"Oink!"

"Justus is okay," I told him. "I missed you," I tried to say, but all that came out was a cough.

I thought the water would shock me when it hit the controller. It didn't. I just stopped. I couldn't feel my fingers. My hands disappeared. My feet. My arms. My body tingled. I heard Jazmine tell me my cells were starved for oxygen. I called to her, but she didn't hear me, she wasn't there. I wasn't anywhere.

I earned a break. Relax. Rest for a second. Everything would be okay.

CHAPTER THIRTY

PIG

Any other time, I would've been thrilled to see Jeremiah.
The flashlight darted around, but I was pretty sure it was
him. He splashed over to me.

*In the event of an emergency, your pig can be used as
a floatation device*, I tried to shout. All that came out was
"Oink."

He gagged. He hugged me for a second and said
the queen was safe. Then the wind stopped. Jeremiah
decided it would be a good time to chill. He let go of me.
The rain stopped. Just like that. The worst of the storm
and then nothing. His head dipped underwater. The
water slowed. He dropped his flashlight. I kicked him.

Help! Fairy Hogmother Saint Emily! Send someone to help! I yelled. Then I heard it. A pig shredder.

ROAR!

It had huge glowing eyes. It got closer and I saw it was a boat with a giant fan on its butt. I already knew about charbroiled pulled-pork sandwiches. I never knew what pulled pork was until I met the shredder. The fan was as tall as a house and covered in shining knives. It roared at us again.

Oh, mighty pig shredder, please spare us! Jeremiah shouldn't go in a sandwich. Only zombies and cannibal girls like Paloma would eat it. Please don't shred us! Sandwich me instead.

It didn't listen. I felt like a dandelion on mowing day. Then I noticed the pig shredder was in a big round cage. I saw that the two boat captains had arrested the pig shredder and locked it up. They stopped the murderous rampage.

A man with a black eye and no beard squatted down and yanked Jeremiah out of the water by his arm. The other tried to pull me onto the boat, but he needed help. Once they got one of my legs inside, I pulled myself in while they strained to lift me.

I flopped into the boat beside a lantern. I rolled over to my brother, but the man with no beard pushed me away and stuck his fingers on Jeremiah's neck. The other guy turned the boat around and talked on the walkie-talkie.

"Yeah, we found the kid. The eye of the storm just moved over us."

The eye of the storm. I didn't know that storms had eyes. If the hurricane had seen how much trouble we were in and had decided to stop, I was glad. They were going to take care of Jeremiah. He was as still and peaceful as the weather. It was a long night, but it was all going to be okay.

The man kneeling over Jeremiah said, "I'm not getting a pulse. We may be too late. Do you know what this machine is?" The next minute was the scariest minute of my life. It took all of my effort to keep myself from running over to Jeremiah and trying to lick him in the face. He had to wake up if I did that. *Please wake up, Jeremiah....*

The man was pushing on his chest, and the other man kept talking into the walkie-talkie.

After less than a minute, we floated over to a huge van with a big red plus sign on the back of it. Mathletes. Maybe they would take Jeremiah to the hospital. Mathletes are smart. They could wake him back up.

All he needs are batteries. If that doesn't work, try licking him, I said.

Some ladies grabbed Jeremiah and tied him onto an orange surfboard and put a blue blanket over his chest and legs.

No! Jeremiah, that's a blue blanket! They're stealing you. These mathletes should have a division sign on their van because they are dividing our family! They are going to take you where they took my other brothers! Come back!

I leapt out of the boat and chased Jeremiah.

GET DOWN OFF THAT SURFBOARD THIS INSTANT! The mathlete kicked at me, and the captains started yelling at me. If they fed me to the pig shredder, I couldn't help anyone.

I'LL FIND YOU, JEREMIAH! I'LL GET HELP AND I'LL SAVE YOU!

I took off running.

I raced through dark streets. I was so glad that they weren't flooded yet. I ran until, for the first time, I was tired of running. The outline of something tall with dim lights in the windows appeared. I made it onto the side-walk. When I got close and ran up the steps, I knew where I was without needing to get a good look. I'd seen this place every week. I might find someone who could help me. I ran into the biggest doors I'd ever seen.

CHAPTER THIRTY-ONE

BOY

I woke staring at freckled ceiling panels and listening to the click of an IV pump.

I tried to focus on the clock in the corner and the sign that said VISITING HOURS 3–7.

My mouth was too dry to talk, but I tried.

"J6?"

Why did I expect him to walk through the door? I felt woozy. Of course he couldn't be here. That's silly. It wasn't three yet. It was dark outside. He'd have to wait for visiting hours to start.

My parents and big sister were lost.

Justus was trapped alone in a flood.

She didn't deserve this. She didn't ruin everything.

I did. I ignored the ICD and ran down the soccer field until my heart stopped. Then I ran out into the storm and did it again. I sat up, but I got too lightheaded and fell back onto my pillow. Light came in through the window, and I could see the whiteboard at the foot of the bed.

RN: KARINA

DOCTOR: CHATTERJEE

PCA: GINNI

PATIENT: UNKNOWN

Everything I did made something worse. Hurt someone. And this was all I had to show for it. Patient: unknown. IVs and electrodes tied me to the hospital bed, but I knew where the nurse button was without having to look.

I told her everything. I told her who I was, what was wrong with me, and where I needed to be. She put the TV on Cartoon Network. I told them my address and all the phone numbers I knew by heart. She said I was very responsible and intelligent for my age. I told her I was twelve. She said I was "very lucky." I didn't show any signs of a "severe site infection" where my driveline went in. Apparently, the EMTs got to me in time. She said there was an angel watching over me. I told her that it was a pig, not an angel. She seemed to think I was loopy on the medication. Then she said she would find my parents if she could. I got a headache. She said I was shaking and asked if I was in pain.

She'd find my parents *if* she could.

If.

I hated them so much for plotting to kill J6. Now I might have hurt my dad and mom. And it didn't matter. J6 was still gone. It was all for nothing.

I turned away from her so she couldn't see me cry a little. She said she'd bring medicine. There isn't any medicine for that.

An hour later, a guy with a beard and a lab coat over his scrubs said I needed a heart transplant and they were trying to get me to the top of the donor list because of how dire my situation was. He said he hadn't heard anything about my family yet, and they were trying to find out which hospital gave me my LVAD so they could contact my normal doctor. I told him about the hospital I usually went to and that I saw Dr. Willis. He gave me pills that might make me sleepy.

It kept me half asleep. Like I was back underwater.

I dreamed Justus showed up again and ran over and gave me a kiss. Mom cried and Dad stood beside

Jazmine. Dad changed the channel to the news. I knew it wasn't real, but some details stood out. Some schools were flooded and others were opening next week. The Dynamos had to cancel the soccer game halfway through. Something about the Cajun Navy. Justus whispered about J6, but he wasn't there. It all went black again.

CHAPTER THIRTY-TWO

PIG

I looked up at a place I'd only seen on Jeremiah's tablet. Church.

SANCTUARY! SANCTUARY! I demand you help me get back to my brother! They took him! I screamed with all the drama I could muster, but once again, all that came out was "Oink!"

The door cracked open, and I ran into a celebrity in pajamas. I used to watch Grandpa-Father Velazquez on the tablet. Now he could help me save Jeremiah.

I nodded politely, then I respectfully bouldered by. He fell on his butt and dropped his flashlight. At least he didn't knock over the table full of candles. I ran between the benches like I was about to get married, but I stopped before I got to the stage. Grandpa-Father closed the elephant-size door behind him, and I followed him to his apartment inside the church.

We were at a farm with this murder-goose and ghost cat, then everything was dark and the queen disappeared, Jeremiah's batteries got in the water, and then the math-letes took him! Help!

I never wanted to explain something as bad as I did right then, but all that came out was "Oink!" I couldn't get stuck here for hours oinking him through every single thing that happened.

"Don't worry. You can stay. I'll figure out what to do with you in a few days. Once everything settles down." He held the flashlight so his face was in shadow, like a true creepy creep. He sounded like he was smiling, but it was a threat.

I didn't need a place to stay. I had a whole house. He wasn't a friend. He was a pignapper! He walked over to the apartment door and shut it.

Click.

I tried to escape. What kind of fortress doesn't have a single piggy door? Grandpa-Father came back with a thick pink blanket that was actually a trap. He folded it and poured water into a bowl. I shivered. He wanted me to get comfortable so I wouldn't try to escape. He wanted me to fall asleep, but I wasn't about to.

I'd just lay down on this blanket to plan my escape and figure out how to find my brother. I turned around five times to check and make sure it was safe. I decided to scheme with my eyes closed. That way I wouldn't be distracted. But whatever I did, I had to stay awake...

According to my stomach, my pignapped pig nap lasted past lunchtime. I leapt off the blanket. Who knows how far away Jeremiah would be by now. I slept half the day. I messed up. He needed me and I wasn't there for him. To find him I'd have to escape. Fast.

When I moved in with Jeremiah, I learned that guests cannot poop or pee on the floor. Or Jazmine's bed. Especially not her pillow. I wasn't even allowed to go in the bathroom, which is where everyone else poops.

No. Guests poop and pee in the yard. That would be my chance. Grandpa-Father took me outside, but the fence was too high to pole-vault. Even if I got free, I didn't know where Jeremiah was. I wanted to cry.

Grandpa-Father made me cereal, but I was hungry for freedom. He poured the milk first. I got scared, because only cereal killers pour the milk first. I had to keep up my strength, so I tried to eat, but the floor was tile, and the bowl was slick on the bottom. It slid. I chased it. The bowl was a better escaper than me. While I was wasting time chasing Froot Loops, Jeremiah was getting farther away.

That night, Grandpa-Father looked down at me while I was planning my escape on my side in the middle of the floor.

He said, "I guess you're just a tired old pig."

I snorted. He thought it was cute to pretend I could hear him. That is called condescending and is considered rude. But then he went into the church and left the door wide open.

However, I didn't jump up and run out the door. What was the point? I'd never find Jeremiah, and maybe I didn't even deserve a brother. It was my fault Jeremiah fell in the water. My fault his batteries got zapped. My fault he got taken by the mathletes to who-knows-where. He did it all for me.

It clicked. He did it all for me. I was thinking about this the wrong way. My brother never gave up on me, so I wouldn't give up on him. Jeremiah messed up constantly, but he was brave and hopeful despite the fact that he's only a human. I have the best that humanity and pigdom have to offer. I'd have to keep going. I eyed the door and stood up.

For Jeremiah! I oinked.

I nosed my way into the huge room with all the benches in it. I froze. People slept on every bench. I'd have to sneak past all of them to get to the door. I was almost there when I smelled something familiar, like a few notes of a song I heard in a commercial once. One blanket lump smelled like body spray and danger. The lump had a picture of guys with different colored hair on it and the letters *BTS*. BTS is short for BITES because it was the girl that bit my brother.

Paloma.

I froze. The zombie girl rolled over, and her braid fell off the side of the bench. I had to get out of here before she got hungry or remembered the incident at Jeremiah's party.

I backed away from her bench and toward the elephant-size door, but then I had an idea. She might know where Jeremiah is. All I'd have to do is espionage. *Espionage* means you spy on someone and follow them, but you're not a creepy stalker. You're a cool spy. Spy movies taught me that if you follow a suspect long enough, they eventually take you exactly where you needed to go. I didn't know anyone who was more of a suspect than a girl who said she ate my brother. Also, she knew Jeremiah. This plan would work. But first I'd need my rest.

I snuck back to bed.

In the morning, Grandpa-Father took me to go to the bathroom by the street in front of the church. I was in some hedges when I saw her. Paloma was on the move. She was walking in a child herd. Maybe they were zombies, too. Zombies often use the buddy system. I didn't want to be anywhere near her, but she might know where Jeremiah was. She might lead me to him.

I danced my happiest dance, I sang my happiest song, and I twerked my twerkiest twerk. I pulled myself together. I was a free pig now, and I knew where I wanted to go.

"Bye, Grandpa-Father!" I ripped the leash out of Grandpa-Father's hands and took off.

All Grandpa-Father heard was "Oink."

CHAPTER THIRTY-THREE

BOY

I woke up and noticed the clock right away. How many nights had I been here? How many nights had I left J6 alone? He wasn't here. But my family was. Maybe. Maybe I dreamed them, but maybe they were in the waiting room.

I couldn't lie down for another second. I kicked the blankets to the ground and pushed the SIT UP and LOWER BED buttons. I untangled the IVs and dropped my feet to the floor. I found a battery and plugged it into the new controller. The hardest part was unplugging the IV pump. I remembered a nurse doing it to help me to a little gray potty beside the bed, but I hadn't reached back there myself.

The IV stand took my weight, and I used it like a cane. I yanked on the latch and opened the door to my room. No nurses were at the station in my cove. I made it into the hallway. The nurse at the bigger station had her back to me. The other one was bent over picking something up.

I had to tell my family I ignored the ICD. They were here. I felt it.

I got lucky. The exit out of the CCU was just one door over. I knew hospitals. I knew the waiting room would be right outside that door, and it would probably have a vending machine that tried to get you to buy green tea.

I shoved that door open, too. I walked past a small sad room with three chairs and a box of tissues. That room was where doctors met with families and told them horrible things. Across the hall, I found the waiting room. The lights were low, and it look me a second to see four shapes.

Justus was cuddled up with Jazmine on a fluffy chair. The other chairs looked uncomfortable, but Mom and Dad were doing their best to sleep in them. Five suitcases I recognized were piled in the corner beside four trash bags. J6 wasn't there.

I sat down next to Dad and shook his shoulder. He took a minute to wake up.

"What are you doing here?" He grabbed me and hugged me from the side. Mom sat up and Justus jumped off Jazmine's lap.

"I'm sorry. I'm so sorry."

"Honey, why aren't you in your room? Come on. You don't look well." Mom stood up.

"Good morning, lazy bones," said Justus. "Now, where is my pig?"

Jazmine shushed her and turned on the light.

I looked at each of their faces. They were worried about me. I tried to take a picture with my mind so I could remember what they looked like when they loved me. I was about to destroy everything.

"I need to tell you something. Bad." Dad tried to hug me, and I pushed him away. Jazmine gave me a tissue. "I'm sorry, Mama. This is my fault." I couldn't look at them. I stared at the tissue. "I'm sorry you had to work a lot. I missed you."

"I've missed y'all these past few months," said Mom.

"Dad, I'm sorry I made you quit your job. And I ran away. Justus, I'm sorry I left you in the attic. I'm sorry J6 is gone."

Jazmine waited for a few seconds for me to say something. Then she coughed and said, "I'll get the nurse."

I took a deep breath. "I felt something before my heart

attack. A few minutes before. I think the ICD zapped me, and I just ignored it. That's why I got sick. That's why you and Dr. Willis got J6 and wanted to…" I looked at Justus and didn't finish that sentence. "That's why you had to quit, Dad. That's why you had to work so much, Mom. I didn't tell you because then you wouldn't…" I covered my face with my hands because my cheeks were getting hot and my head was starting to hurt. "I tricked you all. Then I didn't even follow the list Dr. Willis gave me."

The world spun a little, and I sucked air in and forced it back out. I kept my face covered. This is why people call me a little boy.

Small fingers pried my arms apart. Justus's sweet face looked up at mine.

"You're a crybaby, and you need to stop whining."

"Justus!" said Mom.

"Sorry. Tell us where J6 is. Then you go to your room. Get better. Why did you escape from the hospital room and unplug yourself? Can't you stay one place for one second and not run away?"

"Honey," Mom said to me, "we know about what happened before the game."

"What? No. But I—"

"The ICD records all of your heart functions. We knew as soon as you got to the hospital."

"You knew?"

Dad answered, "Did you think we were going to ground you? You put too much on yourself. It's not all up to you."

"You sound like Jazmine."

"And we"—Mom's voice cracked—"we need you here, Jeremiah. You need to take care of yourself. They just put you on the human transplant list. That means once a person's heart becomes available, you might get it. Promise you'll do better?"

It felt like an unfair thing to ask a bedridden captive, but I said, "I promise. I love you."

"And another thing," Justus said. "The counselor said you need to treat yourself like how you would treat your friends. So, why are you so mean to J6's second-best friend? Why are you mean to my brother? Why can't you just chill out and not run away? See?"

Mom hugged me and said, "We love you no matter what. We'll always love you."

I knew how a human heart "became available." Was I taking up a spot on the list that a little kid like Justus might need?

They hadn't found J6. Was that good or bad? He could be...No, I couldn't even consider that.

Jazmine brought the nurse, and the nurse guided me

back to my room. She tucked me in and turned on the fall alarm so it would alert them if I got out of bed. It didn't go off for the rest of the night.

The next afternoon, Jazmine's phone blew up. But she didn't seem happy about that like she usually was. She seemed really annoyed. Then Dr. Beardface burst into my room.

He said I was stable, there was no infection, and we could go home while we waited for a donor.

Justus turned to Dad. "Where will we go?"

CHAPTER THIRTY-FOUR

PIG

I crept down a street as empty as Jeremiah Five's cushion. When one of the seven kids turned around, I dove into the road. A black van almost pork-chopped me in half, so I did a back handspring into a trash pile. I was following these kids too closely. Luckily, this was the perfect place to hide.

A fridge, pieces of wall, and bags of clothing were heaped up in front of a small white house. I sniffed a chunk of wall that looked like construction paper for dinosaur crafts and had lines going up it like an uneven ruler. The lines were labeled *Claire—2, Claire—3, Claire—4, Claire—5*. Claire was a little kid that grew up in that house and now they were throwing away her growing wall. It smelled like a forgotten closet towel and crumbled when I nosed it. They call it drywall, but it was wet.

I looked up, and the kids were turning a corner. What about their growing walls? Their houses? If this could happen to walls, what about Jeremiah? Was he safe? Paloma was a murderer, but she was also my only lead. I had to keep an eye on her without letting her spot me.

I dashed after them. I made it around the corner and the seven kids had become dozens, or possibly millions waiting outside a one-story building with a fenced-in yard and bushes hugging it. Maybe one of those billions of kids was Jeremiah.

You almost found him! You did it, you beautiful genius! I oinked to myself. I am an excellent encourager. Paloma turned around. I sprang into the bushes. I pushed through stabbing twigs and tickling leaves until my ears stopped me. I froze.

Either these bushes were haunted, or someone was crying. I knew I should follow Paloma sneakily, but I couldn't just leave some ghost sobbing. That's how poltergeist infestations start.

I stealthily stomped forward. The pink-haired DJ girl

that played me music at the farm wiped her puffy eyes. She pushed curls out of her face.

"Backpack Pig? Wow."

I nodded. *Wow* was the appropriate response to me, but I wanted to find Jeremiah. I decided I couldn't leave her sniveling.

"You got lost in the hurricane? Huh? You need to find that little pigboy?"

I nodded.

She picked up her phone, touched the screen a few times, then said, "Where-does-that-little-pigboy-live-question-mark-the-kid-who-passed-out-during-the-game-period. Send."

Her shoulders relaxed. She felt relieved that she figured something out. The phone went back into her pocket. I hoped she was about to take me to my brother. Instead, she grabbed the leash and tied it to a branch before she ran off. What just happened?

How long would she leave me out here? I tried to help her, and this is what I got? I gnawed on the branch. It tasted like vegetables no one had the decency to put ranch on. I turned around and tried to pull the leash over my head. It tightened. I was about to start oinking for my life when she came back.

"*Hey!* Stop. You'll hurt your neck." I stopped. She untied me. "But I can't just leave you here with these clowns."

Clowns! Where?

She ignored me and set down her cardboard plate with apple slices, a milk carton, three tiny pancakes, and two pieces of bacon. She threw me an apple slice, and I caught it in the air. She hunkered down under the bush and picked up the bacon. She held it up to her mouth and looked at me.

"Sorry." She dropped it on the ground. I nodded my approval. I ate two bad pancakes and three apple slices. No one got any bacon because it could be my step-nieces or great-uncles for all I know. Also, I solved the mystery of why Paloma came here. She probably wanted to eat bacon because she's a murderer.

A bell rang, and the girl jumped up. She looked at the building and back at me. She made her decision and pulled me out of the bushes and up to an open door. I had no idea where I was, so I wasn't going in. Most of the kids inside were wearing weird costumes with either green or purple polo shirts and black pants. These must be the clowns she was talking about. They were just junior clowns in training, but they still creeped me out. The costumes were embarrassing. I almost felt bad for them. Almost.

What was this place? It was full of kids, but it was way too loud to be a school. The only thing you could learn here was new cusswords. I pulled back. I wasn't going in there; this place wasn't for me. Paloma would find me here. I couldn't be sneaky. I'm a pig!

I finally realized where I was. A place for mini-clowns: clown college. Not a circus. Circuses have tents and peanut snacks. Clown college is different. It's where clowns learn how to be as scary as the one in the sandwich commercial. Paloma was exactly where she belonged.

A few weeks ago, Justus showed me a movie about a big top and let's just say, it's not great for animals. Elephants are almost twice as strong as I am, and they still get treated worse than Butler Jazmine. I tried to tell the girl that it wasn't safe, but she yanked me inside.

"Get the pig!" and "That's Backpack Pig from Instagram!" I heard. "Kill the pig," I might have also heard. Maybe not. I'm not sure. One trainee clown tried to pull my tail off, but the girl yelled at him.

Everything was brightly colored except the kid's faces. They weren't allowed to wear clown makeup yet; they had to learn to be frightening without it first. They were doing a good job. I thought it couldn't get any worse, but then it was time for the big show. The doors opened and the clowns rushed out of their rooms. I thought they'd do flips or tell jokes. Instead, they must have been trying to kill each other and rip me into little pieces. Or at least scare me to death. I would have been shredded pork, but the girl rushed me into a room. The door slammed shut and trapped me.

The ringmaster was taller than the kids, wore less embarrassing clothes, and held on to a mug like she needed it to live. She stood behind a desk. The room needed more chairs. Most of the kids were eating, and all of them were either screaming quietly or whispering loudly.

"Monica, what are you—" The ringmaster coughed. She choked on the mug liquid.

The girl with the pink hair was named Monica.

Monica yelled louder than the other clowns, "Miss, we need to find out where this pig lives. She's lost."

Monica called me *she* even though I have it on good authority that I'm probably a boy.

"I'll have someone come get it." Ringmaster Miss texted someone.

Hands shot up and heads turned toward me.

"But, Miss, it's Backpack Pig," said a boy. He pointed so no one would be confused about the only pig in the room.

"The school director is coming in a few minutes."

"Miss!" another kid called out, "They're looking for a pig. Some of the kids from Coleman were talking about it. That's the Instagram Pig."

"Also, he wrecked the food festival. It was awesome."

"Everyone, take a seat or line up in the back if you don't have anywhere to sit. Hopefully everyone from Coleman will be able to go back to their school soon once they make whatever repairs...Um, Yaritza, will you take that pig outside and let it go? Here's a hall pass. Joey! Put those scissors down. Please, take your seat. Or stand over there. Carlos, pass out the books. Joey, I'll get you a Band-Aid, did you get your blood on your neighbor? Yaritza—"

One mini-clown stole a red pen, turned around, and slashed another kid's arm until I could see a red line of blood. Another threw a paper. Two started sneaking toward me.

A girl with short hair walked carefully over to Monica like she was afraid of being bitten. Monica gave her *a look*, and the girl sat back down. Then a phone chimed.

"Monica, you need to keep your phone on silent in class, but I understand if there's some different circumstances today, just, umm—"

Monica turned to me. "Some kid, Pamela or something,

just answered on the soccer league's WhatsApp. I got little pigboy's address. I owe him one. I gotta go."

She stood up and pulled me toward the door. The ringmaster rushed over and put her hand on Monica's shoulder. Monica jerked like it hurt her.

"Monica, take your seat."

"Don't touch me."

"Is everything all right? Is your family okay?"

"None of your business."

"Is your house—"

"Stop!"

Everyone finally got quiet. Then she cried. She ran into the hall. I could barely keep up.

She exploded out a door and collapsed onto the steps outside the building. She took off her hoodie and balled it up. She stuck it over her mouth and screamed. Good thing I'm a health care and educational expert.

"I'm just so mad all the time..."

"Oink." It was all I needed to say. I laid my head down on her knee and offered her the privilege of scratching my adorable noggin. It was the greatest honor I could bestow. After a few scratches, she was hooked. She scooted down another step, hugged my neck.

"I might get suspended, but I'll take you home."

I nodded and danced.

"Ms. Wang hates me."

I shook my head no. I let her hug me.

"I don't know why I get so angry. I hope your house is okay."

I wondered if Monica had a growing wall in her yard, too.

Yes, but I don't need the leash, you know. I'm a grown pig that makes his own decisions now, I said, but all she heard was "Oink."

We went three blocks until I recognized the Oasis Market. I was so excited. I broke into a run, and she dropped the leash. I knew the way home from here! I stopped and turned around. I oinked at Monica. She smiled before she turned back.

CHAPTER THIRTY-FIVE

BOY

My house was gone.

"You're being a little bit dramatic," Mom told Justus. "The house is there, but we'll need to find a place to stay until we're done cleaning it up. Maybe we'll move. Jazmine, can you call that hotline again? The one on the card the nurse gave us? See if you can find us a hotel. Take Justus."

Jazmine looked at the doctor. She had a list of questions. She usually seemed like she knew more about what was going on with me than the doctors did. She wanted to be in the room for the conversation, but she left holding Justus's hand.

"Jeremiah is stable enough to go, but he'll need to

keep off his feet. I saw in his chart that he's part of a clinical trial and already slated to receive a donor organ?" said the doctor.

"I was. From a pig. But the pig died in the hurricane. He drowned in the water. He didn't have a pulse. He definitely died. I need to get on the human waiting list."

"Are you sure he's gone?" asked Dad.

"Yes." If he were still alive, I hoped my lie was good enough to keep him safe.

Jazmine and Justus got back. None of the hotels had any vacancies. Apparently, the mattress store was letting people stay there, as well as my church, but that wouldn't work. Jazmine's phone buzzed, and she answered it hopefully.

"Hello...No, you can't talk to him right now. Bye... My house is none of your business. I need to talk to the doc—How did you know the hospital? How is it you always just show up where you are not invited? There's a thing called manners....Ugh. Fine. I can't even with you."

The annoying person on the other end wouldn't let up. She trudged back out the door.

Justus turned to Mom. "Where are we going to stay?"

I saw her and my first thought was that this was my fault. Then I challenged it. What would J6 think of me? He would know the hurricane wasn't actually my fault. He wouldn't know what caused it. He'd have some wild explanation involving canes or dinosaurs, but he wouldn't blame me for it. Not everything was about me, and maybe I didn't have to fix everything.

Maybe I needed to see the counselor that Justus mentioned when I went back to school. Or talk to Father Velazquez. I needed help with these feelings.

I needed something.

Jazmine opened the door again. "School's out."

Adnan pushed past her and ran to my bed.

"I told her that we didn't need to bring these bags. We should have left them in my dad's car because we're all going to the same place anyway. But this makes us look like Trash Santa."

"What are you talking about? Who else is here?" I asked.

Paloma dragged a trash bag behind her. Adnan's dad, Farid, came in carrying the other one.

"She wouldn't leave me alone until I called your sister and found out where you were." Adnan pointed his thumb at Paloma. She didn't have Jazmine's number.

Paloma saw me in the hospital bed and froze. She looked away and picked up her bag. She set it at my feet.

My parents started talking to Adnan's dad when Paloma leaned over to my face. I honestly thought she was going to kiss me. Right in front of everyone.

She didn't. She whispered, "My house got flooded. So did our school."

"I'm so sorry."

"That's not important now. My family's staying at the church. That's near Jemison Middle. I went there today."

"You went to school?"

"Adnan didn't, but I did. My parents wanted me to, and they have breakfast and lunch. Anyway, all of Coleman is going there until they can fix our school, and the kids say that they saw a pig. Monica from soccer asked the WhatsApp chat where you lived and I told her. I think she took J6 to your house. I saw her talking to the guidance counselor later. She probably got in trouble or something. J6 is safe."

"He's a fighter."

"And a biter."

Paloma pulled away, and Adnan looked embarrassed. "Paloma, I get my dad to drive you here, you harass an innocent evil sister and lug this bag all the way through the hospital, and now you whisper sweet nothings? I have secrets, too."

Adnan leaned over me and whispered, "We brought you some clothes and stuff. Do you want to stay at my house?"

"Yeah! Dad, can we stay with Adnan?"

"Farid and I were just talking about that. It would be perfect. And thank them for the supplies. We'll head over to their place. Then tomorrow afternoon we can check out our house and see what we can do."

Wait, J6 is at my house waiting for me, and Dad wants to head over there tomorrow afternoon? I didn't have much time.

I still felt numb. J6 was alive. And he was looking for me. Why did he go home? He needed me. I needed to get to him before my parents did. He was probably just lonely. I needed to save him from saving me.

I wasn't going to make the same mistakes I made last time I ran away. I couldn't disappear without telling anyone. And it was getting dark. I wasn't going tonight. I was going to be careful.

I called the Rescue Ranch hotline and asked to talk to Emily. Then I told Adnan my plan. Well, everything except for where J6 was. If he checked WhatsApp, he'd figure it out, but he hadn't yet. He told me I should tell my parents. The door swung open.

Jazmine stood there like a prison guard. I wished that she'd go back to Adnan's sister's room.

"I heard you. You found the pig and now you want to run away again. Tomorrow morning? Tell me where he is." She said "he," not "it."

I shook my head no.

She gave Adnan a look. He didn't budge. She turned back to me. "Do you know the odds of finding a compatible heart donor in time?"

"In time for what?"

"You damaged your heart going after that pig. You need this transplant. As soon as possible. Tell me where he is."

"What are you talking about?"

"If you don't get a new heart…it will be really bad for you. Please tell me what you know."

I was already supposed to use a wheelchair. I already had the list that didn't want me to cross my legs or sit or stand. "Go away. I'm fine."

"No, Dr. Chatterjee told us that…" She turned away from me. Adnan stared at her.

Then he said, "I think the doctor said you're dying."

Jazmine climbed over a mound of dirty clothes and stood in Adnan's corner.

Killing J6 to save myself was the same as killing Justus or Jazmine. He needed me. That doctor didn't know me. He didn't know J6 and didn't understand. Sometimes I got sick, but I'd be fine.

Jazmine wiped her eyes and turned back around. "Do you care about us at all?"

I was too angry to answer her.

CHAPTER THIRTY-SIX

PIG

The houses on my street used to have yards and fences and toys out front. One guy had a car's dead body in his yard, but besides that they were clean. What happened? The houses all had their mouths open like a pig without the apple. All their guts splattered on the grass: furniture, walls, piles of carpet.

I sprinted home.

Pigs aren't just beautiful. Our bodies are perfectly aerodynamic, making us the fastest creatures on the earth. Zebras seem fast because they have racing stripes, and cheetahs have bad sportsmanship, but pigs are faster than either of them.

One house didn't have trash all over the yard. One

house didn't have a creepy open door. One house seemed safe. I was home.

JEREMIAH! I screamed for my brother, but no one answered. He'd be inside. And Queen Justus would be there. Maybe she'd run out and greet me like she did when we first met.

I rammed the door. Locked. I did it again, and the doorframe broke. The door creaked open. I had no idea how strong I was. Or how mushy the doorframe would be.

I stood in the opening, expecting to see my family. Instead, I froze. The house was all wrong.

The carpet had become a slime factory. I couldn't tell what color it was supposed to be, and it was so nasty I could almost taste the germs from outside. And that was the carpet I could see. Most of it was covered in books and clothes and trash. The storm had hit the house. Queen Justus was right again. My home filled up with dirty gray water and left all of its nastiness behind.

I'd faced that smell before. Jeremiah threw a drippy towel into his closet because the laundry basket was full and he was gross. He forgot about it and covered it in dirty clothes and popped soccer balls. That towel eventually became haunted by a stinky ghost. I went in there one time and smelled it. It had been in there for weeks but it never dried. The house smelled like it was made out of closet towels. I stepped inside.

Squish. The carpet smushed and oozed around my feet. *Splash. Squish. Splash. Squish.* Every time I stepped, my home tried to suck me in. The couch where I saved Jeremiah from Paloma looked like a zombie couch. The fabric was torn and rotted and even the bugs on it didn't want to stay.

Butler Jazmine's crate was covered in goo. I couldn't even go into the kitchen where I'd eaten my oatmeal. Dad's plan to save the food in the fridge didn't work. The door was open and the meat inside rotted.

I ran into Justus's room. Mr. Stinky Bear and Professor Fuzzy Shark had both run away. At least the shark can swim. I wasn't sure my family was gone until I noticed Jazmine had taken her cell phone charger. Finally, I went to our room.

Why did Jeremiah have to run into the water? He was not a floatation device. I thought the mathletes saved him. If they did, he should be back by now.

I counted. The first night the mathletes took him. I spent two nights with Grandpa-Father, and he wasn't back yet. He grabbed me, told me Justus was okay, and then he sank.

JEREMIAH! I screamed so loud I almost heard myself say the right thing instead of "Oink!"

I ran to his machine and rammed the TV tray it sat on. It crashed to the floor. It was still plugged in, but it was dead.

Was my brother okay?

Dear Fairy Hogmother Saint Emily, please save my brother. I'll do anything if you can make sure he's okay. Please.

My family was gone. My sisters. My parents. My brother. All gone.

The room made me want to throw up, but I couldn't leave. I wiggled into Jeremiah's bed and tried to fall asleep in a little puddle. I'd always wondered what a water bed was. I didn't get the hype. Maybe when I woke up, my brother would be back. Maybe he'd never be back. I'd wait for him. I'd wait as long as it took.

CHAPTER THIRTY-SEVEN

BOY

Adnan's windows faced the wrong way, his nightlight cast demented shadows, and his pillow smelled too clean. But I was happy. I was pretty sure I knew where J6 was. And I got a bed. I wanted a phone. I needed to look something up. Adnan's was on the nightstand charging about a foot from me. I didn't touch it.

It was an hour until 8:30 a.m. An hour until my plan started. Adnan snored on a leaky blow-up mattress beside me. I watched him slowly sink into the floor. When he was almost flat on the ground, he jumped up.

The first thing he did was check the powerbase on his desk. It was lit up, so he followed the power cord to me.

"I'm just making sure. So you woke up and decided to stare at me like a creepy robot?"

"I'm a nice robot."

"No such thing. Well, why don't you creep on Instagram instead? Wait, do you need help with something?"

Before I could answer, he stood up the air mattress and kicked his clothes mounds into one big pile at the side of his room. He made a path for me.

"There. Now you're free. Do you need help with anything else?"

"I want to creep on Instagram."

"I knew it."

He chucked his phone at me. I opened his Instagram and almost immediately found what I was looking for: a boomerang of J6. When those kids recorded him, I had no idea anyone would care about it. J6 drew the smiley face in the dirt hundreds of times before I even noticed that fifty thousand other people had watched him do the same thing. A different post had sixty thousand views, but the smiley face captured him best. Adnan found some clean clothes in his closet and took them to the bathroom.

I could use this to prove that he's smart. I could show Emily and Dr. Willis.

I scrolled through the comments on J6's video for the first time.

FutureMrsJJWatt She's a girl. See the backpack?
4d • 12 likes • reply

Caseylovesgoldfish He was at the field trip. Everyone saw him.
4d • 2 likes • reply

EmilyFights4animals What field trip? Where?
3d • like • reply

Caseylovesgoldfish Jemison Middle.
3d • like • reply

EmilyFights4animals What does his tattoo say? Does it say "Gen-e-heart"?
3d • like • reply

FutureMrsJJWatt Who are you @EmilyFights4animals? Are you off that commercial? #strangerdanger
3d • 5 likes • reply

Caseylovesgoldfish BACKPACK PIG CAME TO OUR SCHOOL TODAY.
18hr • 15 likes • reply

My heart felt lighter.

Adnan came back, fully dressed.

"I read the WhatsApp message. You need to tell them where to find J6."

"You know I can't."

"I know you think this is your fault. I know you feel guilty. That's okay. But..." For the first time, Adnan didn't know what to say. But he was wrong. I knew it wasn't my fault. That's not why I had to save J6.

"I can't do that. He's my brother," I said.

But Adnan didn't see it that way. I wanted to make him swear he'd keep my secret. Swear it or we weren't friends. But that didn't feel right. He knew my whole plan, but I couldn't ask him to lie for me. I just looked at him.

"There's an eighty percent chance that I'll rat you out to your parents if they ask me where you are," he said.

"Then I'll hurry."

"You better. I won't cover for you. At all. You might die. That's what Jazmine said."

I noticed he didn't make any jokes because this time he wasn't trying to make me feel better. He wanted to scare me enough to change my mind.

"J6 isn't a normal pig. He's smart like a person. Did you know that he has a human heart? Well, I think he has a human brain, too. I'm not doing this because I feel bad about what I did." It was because I loved him.

"I don't care." Adnan loved me, too.

Adnan helped me with my battery pack. He dug through his clothes and tried to find some shorts or pants that would fit, but they were all too big and he couldn't find a belt. He and Paloma must have known that, because Paloma gave me a pair of her jeans. My hands couldn't fit into the pockets. Adnan's shirts didn't squeeze my driveline, and his big hoodie fit over the battery.

I poked my head out the door. I was afraid I'd wake up Mom, Dad, or Justus in the living room. Instead, I almost smacked into Jazmine. I'd left my wheelchair out there last night. Now it was gone.

"Wait here. I'm taking you."

"No. You'll tell Mom and Dad. Or Dr. Willis."

"How can I do that if I don't know where we're going? Get back in, and I'll get your chair."

I only had twenty minutes to get to the house. When I called her last night, Emily said, "Eight thirty sharp." It was already 8:10. Jazmine went all the way across the house and took another five minutes to get back with the wheelchair. What was she doing?

"I'm going on my own."

"Get in. Trust me. At least let me watch out for you. You owe me this."

I didn't have a choice. She pushed me out the door. I asked to hold on to her phone so I could check the time, but she wouldn't let me. She was texting someone.

CHAPTER THIRTY-EIGHT

PIG

I could barely hear the sound that woke me up. In my dream it was the horn on my custom Bugatti. Jeremiah and I moved into our own mansion. Did he expect me to walk all the way from the breakfast burrito room to the home theater? Not a chance. My car's horn reminded me of Jazmine's ringtone. My heart knew what it was before my head did.

"J," a voice outside whispered. I took a deep breath in. I was probably imagining things.

"Six."

I jumped out of bed and ran to the front door.

There he was. Finally.

Jeremiah sat in the doorframe. He focused on his

breathing and every few seconds he'd glance behind him. I hoped he'd become a spy and gone into hiding. I'd hoped the wheelchair was actually some kind of submarine plane. But no. He was sick. He was wearing new clothes. I tried to notice anything about him besides what was most obvious.

He wasn't happy to see me. Something was wrong.

He took calm breaths. I ran over to him and stuck my nose into his side. He leaned over toward me. I sniffed his face. If he smelled good, I'd have been really worried, but he smelled normal instead. I gave him a minute. He sat up. He moved his hand toward me like he was about to scratch behind my ears. Then he snapped it away like I was a cannibal girl about to devour him.

"I called the ranch. They're coming to get you in a few minutes. I need you to go with them." He talked slowly. He looked inside his house, and his eyes opened wider. His mouth didn't close, and he leaned back. He didn't know what had happened. Everyone else had cleaned out their houses and piled all the ruined stuff out front. He hadn't been back. That's why there was no trash in the yard. He rolled away from the doorframe. I went outside.

Jazmine stood on the sidewalk talking on the phone. I had heard it ring. As soon as I stepped outside, she turned the phone away from me and hid it. She stared at the street like she was a lookout during a bank robbery. I went back inside.

"They're going to get me another heart," Jeremiah said. "I don't need yours. They'll find one from a human donor."

Then I remembered what Dr. Willis said about my heart. My heart was his best chance. That's the same thing Jazmine's book said.

He stood up and used the walls to support himself. He needed me more than ever. He squished through the living room and peeked out the window.

As soon as he did that, I heard something stop in front of my house. Doors opened and closed. Then someone stepped through the front door.

I looked up at Fairy Hogmother Saint Emily standing in the doorway with the light coming in from behind her and a beautiful flowing T-shirt. The canvas sleeves on her jacket looked like angel wings. She had a tattoo of a pig inside of a heart on her wrist. Her face shined as beautiful as a candle. Then she saw me. Her smile spread across her face brighter than a burning cake. She dropped to her knees, and they splashed in the carpet, but she didn't care. The first thing she did was grab my head and kiss the top of it. Then she scratched behind my ears and stared at me like how Justus stares at pizza.

"Wow. You're special."

"He's from Gen-e-heart. They messed with his DNA. He was born just so they could kill him."

"I've been trying to get something on them for a few years now. But that's not why I'm most excited to meet you. I just liked your dancing." She laughed and I did a little shuffle for her.

She turned to Jeremiah.

"He understood me!"

I nodded.

"At the ranch our pigs get all sorts of visitors. But you're not going to live at the ranch."

I backed up and cocked my head to the side.

"No, you seem like you'd rather stay at my house. And Jeremiah could visit you whenever you wanted. Would you like that?"

An instant promotion. I nodded my head as hard as I could. Jeremiah smiled. It was everything I ever wanted, but I wasn't sure about leaving Jeremiah. I was born to be his brother and stay by his side. But I was also born so that Dr. Willis could steal my heart.

"Come on. Let's go." Fairy Hogmother Saint Emily

opened the door, and I followed her outside. Her friend was talking to Jazmine and opened the van. A platform lowered to the ground. I froze.

Come on, legs. Walk into the van, I said, but all my legs heard was "Oink."

"Don't be afraid," said Jeremiah. He walked back out and sat in his wheelchair. "Don't worry about me."

I looked at Jazmine. She shook her head no. I'd never seen her look like that. She was trying to tell me about Jeremiah. He wasn't doing well. And she knew I would understand because he's her brother, too. She knew I was smart, and she did not think I should go with Fairy Hogmother Saint Emily.

"Go ahead, I'm okay," Jeremiah said.

Jeremiah was not okay. Not at all.

More than just me and Jazmine, Jeremiah knew it, too. Fairy Hogmother Saint Emily was the only one who didn't know. Jeremiah wanted me to get into the van and leave him.

I'm serious, legs, walk! I tried to get them to move, but they still wouldn't. They were listening to my heart and my heart wasn't working right. My brain told me to climb into the van and begin my life as a fashionable yet relatable hero. Jeremiah would visit me at the ranch in his wheelchair. Maybe. But my heart kept beating the same rhythm. My pigheartedness shouted at me, louder than ever before: *brother*.

Jeremiah knew he might die, but he still wanted me to go. But it wasn't up to him. I was too big for anyone to carry, so no one could make me do anything. I spent most of my life thinking that pigs didn't get to decide anything, but I found out that I was a very good decider. I was born to give him my heart, but that didn't matter. I chose to become his brother. Dr. Willis didn't own me. Not even Jeremiah owned me. No one got to choose what I did but me.

And no one was going to steal my heart.

I was going to give it away. Every beat in my pigheartedness led me to Jeremiah. And no one, not even my brother, could stop me.

CHAPTER THIRTY-NINE

BOY

J6 held his head a little higher, but he wasn't moving. He already knew what he was going to do, and I couldn't let him. Jazmine stood at the edge of the yard like she was still waiting for someone. She put her phone back in her pocket.

"You need to go. Please. For me," I said. "I'm fine."

J6 shook his head no.

"Come here, buddy. Come on," said Emily.

J6 needed to understand. He needed to leave. He looked perfectly calm. Confident.

"Don't stay for me. I'm sicker now. Because of you. I don't want your heart. Go away."

J6 walked up to me.

"I hate you," I said.

He nuzzled me. He'd made up his mind. He oinked and I knew what he was trying to say. I wanted to tell him I loved him, too.

"GET IN THE VAN!" I tried to push him away, but I hit his neck. He walked closer and licked my hand.

I'm so sorry, little brother. I love you so much is what I wanted to say, but what came out was "You made me sick. You're stupid. You're bad for me. And the house is ruined forever because you made me leave. Now we have nowhere to live. It's your fault. I don't love you. Leave. Now."

He nodded, turned around, and walked over to Jazmine.

I wanted to scream at him. My words didn't come out. I wanted to pick him up, throw him into the van, and slam the door, but I couldn't. I could barely breathe.

He looked up at Jazmine and nodded. She seemed surprised. Like a pig just nodded at her. *"NO!"* I screamed. I stood up and started across the yard.

Jazmine ignored me. She told Emily, "His doctor is on her way. You need to go."

How could I hate him and love him so much at the same time? I did everything for him, and he was throwing it away.

I had to do something. I dug Adnan's too-big sneakers into the grass and stumbled, but I kept going. I fell before I made it halfway across the yard.

J6 ran over to me and rested his head on the heart that wasn't beating. I felt his. This couldn't be the last time I felt his heartbeat. He looked at me and it reminded me of when Justus was little, but I couldn't just sit here and hold him. I tried to shove him off me, but he was too strong.

"Emily, please. Please take him. Save him. Please."

J6 shook his head no.

Emily looked at me and said, "I'm so sorry. It looks like he made his decision." She wiped her eyes.

"No. Come back!" She didn't turn around. She climbed into her van with her assistant and pulled away.

I'd lost everything. I'd lied and risked it all, but I still failed. I pulled J6 close.

No. I wouldn't give up on him. This wasn't the end. I wouldn't let it be. He still had a chance. He could hide. He could run.

I tried to find somewhere for him to go. I still had time.

"Please. Just please go through the neighbor's yard. For me."

He wanted to sit with me. I wanted to be with him,

too, but spending time together now meant we'd miss out on years together later. Then I had an idea.

"You can hide out until the coast is clear," I whispered. "Then I'll come find you at the co-op farm. You know the way. They won't notice you. We still have time."

That would work. I didn't know my plan until I said it, but there was real hope. This wasn't good-bye. I'd get to keep my brother. I smiled and finally felt like I could relax. J6 looked at my face carefully, and stood up. He looked down the street, planning where he was going to hide. He decided to stay alive for me. He decided we wouldn't give up on each other. I felt like I did the night of the hurricane when I realized we'd missed the soccer game and J6 was safe.

But he didn't start walking. He just stared down the street. I turned my head and saw Adnan's car. J6 didn't know what it looked like, so what was he looking at?

A second later I spotted it. A silver Gen-e-heart van barreling down the road right behind it.

Mom and Dad got to the house right before Dr. Willis.

I turned angrily to Jazmine. "You promised you wouldn't call anyone." I looked at J6. "I thought we'd have more time. I needed more time."

Before, it felt like five minutes with him was nothing.

Now it was everything.

After he was gone, I'd give anything to have him back. Anything to see him again. Anything for an extra minute. Even though I'd never been more miserable, this was still the happiest I would be for a long time, and Jazmine stole our time away. She stole his future.

She couldn't look at me.

"I trusted you!"

The van parked and Dr. Willis stepped out. She ran over to me. An orderly stepped out of the driver's side door. He walked around to the side of the van and opened it. He climbed inside and came out with what looked like a long stick with a loop at the end.

Mom and Dad ran over to me, too. Dad looked at me, and looked at the pig. Mom and Dad knew I lied again. But they lied. So did Jazmine. My head hurt. I couldn't deal with them right now. Dad tried to help me stand.

"Let me go! I hate you!" I screamed. J6 looked over at me. He shook his head.

"You need a new heart. Right away," said Dr. Willis. "Your parents can drive you to the hospital."

"You want to kill him. Murderer!"

I kicked, but it didn't help. I looked just like a baby. A little boy.

"J6! RUN! HIDE!" I screamed. Maybe he'd be okay. Maybe there was still the tiniest bit of hope.

Jazmine walked over to me and turned to Dr. Willis.

"Just so you know, the pig wants to do this," she said. Dr. Willis looked down at J6 and he nodded his head.

She looked horrified. "But how...?"

My last hope. "There's another way," I said. "There's another option. Please."

Dr. Willis shook her head no. "You need his heart," she said very quietly.

"We need to do this. This will save your life," Jazmine said. "I know he's special, but he's just a pig."

"He's my brother."

"And you're my brother."

CHAPTER FORTY

PIG

Jeremiah was my brother. He needed a heart with strong ventricle walls, and he needed it now. Dr. Willis said so herself, even though I didn't need her to. Jazmine's face told me everything I needed to know.

I thought I wanted out of room 23. I thought I wanted to find Fairy Hogmother Saint Emily. I thought I wanted that more than anything, but I guess I didn't. I wanted more time with Jeremiah. So did Jazmine. I pulled away from him. He seemed weak before, but he held on tight. I looked up at her.

I'm sorry for pooping on your bed. It was really funny. I hope Jeremiah promotes you. To me, you're more than just a butler. You're the head butler.

She stared at me, and she understood. She nodded her head. I was pretty sure I only said, "Oink." But she knew. My sister didn't chase me. She let me walk back to Jeremiah and put my head on his foot. I laid down.

She looked at me, really looked at me for the first time. It felt kind of creepy, so I stuck my tongue out at her. She blinked and seemed spooked. Maybe she didn't know I was smarter than the average pig?

"Go stand by the mailbox," she whispered.

The mailbox was a few feet in front of the Gene-heart van, but I did what she said and her mouth fell open. Then I walked to the van door. I turned to my Mom and Dad. "I'm sorry you'll have to live without me."

I wanted to say good-bye to Jeremiah. I nosed him in the leg, but he cried and screamed at me.

Listen, I have important stuff to say to you, I said. He was yelling at me so loud he couldn't hear what I needed to say.

This is our last time together. Listen to me! It wasn't any use. I thought of something I'd heard in a movie. *Sometimes to help someone, you have to let them go. Unless they're hanging off a skyscraper*, I told him.

He just kept screaming, but Dad understood me. He picked Jeremiah up and carried him to the car. My family drove away. It was just Dr. Willis and me. Just like in the beginning. I climbed into her van and she sat with me. She just wanted to help Jeremiah, too. I thought I could finally trust her.

The door shut, and she stabbed me in my hams.

What would happen *after* the surgery?

Would I see Jeremiah again? Would it be like I'm asleep without dreaming? What about Jeremiah? He was a wreck before. He cried all the time and kept getting himself into trouble, but maybe my heart was a little stronger. Maybe it'd do a better job for him. Maybe he just needed strong ventricle walls. I told myself to be strong. I told myself I had to be a good brother for the rest of my life. That shouldn't be too hard since it wouldn't last long.

As soon as the door opened, Dr. Willis lowered the ramp, and I took little steps. My legs weren't very fast, but Jeremiah's heart was racing in my chest and pushing me forward. The parking lot still felt like the surface of the moon, and everyone I knew was millions of miles away.

She used her key to take me into the long hallway, but she kept looking back at me.

When I left room 23 months ago to be with

Jeremiah, it had felt like I was floating away from my world. Walking back into that building now was like falling into a hole.

The hallway she took me down was shorter than the one I left.

I didn't pick up my head.

When I got back to my cell, Dr. Willis turned on my TV. Room 23 wasn't as big as it used to be. I didn't face my TV or watch my shows. I stared at the wall.

I was alone and without my brother. This time, I knew I'd never see him again. The last time he touched me was a push instead of a hug. One of the last things he said to me was that he hated me. He was trying to save me, even if it meant he would die. I wished I could see him just one more time.

CHAPTER FORTY-ONE

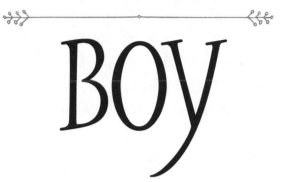

BOY

When I woke up, no one was there. I looked out the huge window. I could see the Gen-e-heart logo next door. I felt dizzy, but I kicked my legs over the side of the bed. I almost puked. I stood up, but the floor rocked like a boat.

I had to walk out of here. I couldn't use my wheelchair. That would look suspicious. I held my gown closed in back and stood. Then I fell and twisted so I landed on my back and didn't hit my driveline. I stared through the open door at a red EXIT sign…

Jazmine woke me up. I was back in my bed.

"Your surgery is scheduled in a few hours."

My brain fuzzed. I wished Adnan or Paloma were here.

They'd help me. Well, maybe not Adnan. He's too good of a friend. "I got you back in bed before anyone found you," Jazmine said. "Mom and Dad are finishing your paperwork. We don't have a lot of time." She plugged in my battery pack. Then she leaned over and picked me up.

"I hate you."

"Shut up." She dropped me into a wheelchair.

"Traitor—" I couldn't finish before she put her finger on my lips.

"Trust me."

That's what I did last time, and she killed my brother.

She pushed me down the hall and into an elevator. The nurses were busy. They didn't notice her.

In three hours, they would murder my only brother because I didn't do enough to save him.

No. J6 wouldn't want me to think like that. He never thought like that. He loved me. How could I treat someone J6 loved like garbage?

She pushed me past MEDICAL PERSONNEL ONLY doors.

"Wait, stop!"

She didn't. She leaned over and whispered, "This hallway connects us to Gen-e-heart. It's how they take the pigs to the operating theater." Theater? I imagined being up on stage while the doctors cut me in half and made J6 disappear. Like a terrifying magic show. "I found it while you were sleeping. I also talked to Dr. Willis when she checked your vitals and then left her lab coat on a chair. I'm not sure that she'll want to keep mentoring me."

We heard someone coming down the hallway, so she used Dr. Willis's key card and pushed me into the first room on the right.

The room was completely white. There were three wheeled stainless-steel tables with pigs strapped to them and IV pumps and medical equipment set up beside them. Two of the pigs had intubation tubes snaking out of their throats. Jazmine left me by the door and walked over to look at them.

"They do animal testing, so this must be the—"

"Recovery room." I'd woken up from enough surgeries to know exactly where I was. J6 was never going to end up here.

I felt a fresh wave of anger. Jazmine stared at the monitor of the pig closest to the door.

"This little piggy isn't doing too good."

His chest was stitched up and like the others he was heavily sedated. For a minute I almost thought he was J6. They were practically identical.

I wheeled myself closer and reached out to touch his side. It was warm and fuzzy, like J6's. His breathing was ragged and I wasn't sure if he could even feel me, but I gave him a few scratches.

"I'm so sorry." And then I thought about what the doctors were trying to do with all of these pigs in this research hospital. "And thank you."

Thanking him couldn't make up for how wrong all of this felt.

Jazmine grabbed a stethoscope off the back of a chair and held it up to the door.

"The coast is clear. Come on."

We went down an elevator and ended up in a really long hallway that seemed to lead outside.

She stopped in front of a door labeled ROOM 23.

"So much for my future in medicine." She pulled Dr. Willis's ID out of her pocket and held it in front of the card reader. The light turned green. She opened the door. We stepped inside, and the alarm went off. It must be to prevent pigs from escaping.

WEE WEE WEE.

My brother lay still in a plastic enclosure next to five empty ones. He looked like he was already dead.

WEE WEE WEE.

Jazmine pulled my wheelchair back and turned it around. I jumped out and dashed for him.

"We got to go. They know we're here. Say your goodbyes quick."

I opened his pen. He was there. Real. Safe. I hugged him. Four people crowded in.

"STOP!" I shrieked. I was crying again, like a little boy, but I didn't hide it. I didn't care what anyone thought. My feelings were the same feelings J6 had. They were normal. I could cry.

"You can't." I sucked air in. "Killers." Wheeze. Inhale. "Mistake."

I let him go.

"RUN!"

I turned to the adults who had just come in. *J6 has a human brain. He looks like a pig, but he's a kid, just six months old. The doctors made him out of me, and J6 taught me how to be a better brother and person. He saved me, and he loves me. He has my heart, but he has his own soul. You can give me that heart, but it won't do any good. I love him.* I tried to say that, but all that came out was "love."

My world blurred. Instead of running away, my brother headbutted me gently.

"Oink."

"Jeremiah. He wants to do this. They didn't catch him. He was trying to get back to you. He understands," whispered Jazmine. J6 nodded.

For the first time I really looked at my sister. She had tears in her eyes. She was right. He wanted to give me his heart. The only problem was, he already had mine.

CHAPTER FORTY-TWO

PIG

I dreamed Jeremiah got better. I would help him through school. We'd go to Rice University together. They'd let me attend his soccer games and classes because I am a medical professional. He'd earn degrees in soccer and hair-growing, or whatever he's interested in when he's eighteen. Maybe theater? I'd be at his graduation. They'd let me walk with him across the stage and hold his diploma for him. That would be a big crowd-pleaser.

He goes on to be a professional soccer player, or an actuary, or a barista. He'll have studied so hard that he'll become a doctor who can help kids with heart problems or a scientist who builds a laser that could destroy the moon because he doesn't like how it looks at him. By then Jazmine will be a billionaire, so maybe we'll be her butlers.

I would help him with his work, keep him on the straight and narrow, and finally introduce him to someone he could marry. Maybe Paloma or Adnan. Even though she might bite me and he's a bit much. Most couples can't go out because they need babysitters. Not Jeremiah and Ms. or Mr. Jeremiah. I would watch the kids and tutor them. The kids would be named J8, J9, and J10. Jeremiah gets to keep J7 for himself. They would go to college, and I would retire when Jeremiah does. We'd go live in some tropical island paradise (not Hawaii, I don't care for luaus) and visit the grandkids. That's the kind of life we could have. That'd be perfect. I'd be in hog heaven.

I woke up, and Dr. Willis was helping three butlers pick me up and put me on the Magic Table. The blue blanket was warm. Not scary.

They wheeled me through the hallway. It was the closest I'd ever come to my Bugatti. I'd been arrested and to the farm, church, and school, but I had never been to a hospital. I was the picture of health.

In the hall, I saw my family. Jazmine walked over to me and whispered, "Thank you." I nodded. She left the room. Justus gave me a kiss, but she didn't know what was going to happen. I told them goodbye. Mom patted my head, and Dad cried a little.

They wheeled me down the hall and into a big plain room with two tables in the middle. Jeremiah was waiting for me.

Four nurses moved me onto the operating table beside Jeremiah. It reminded me of the first night I snuck into his room. Dr. Willis scratched my belly, but she got something in her eye and had to turn away from the other doctors and clean her face.

The stabbers came back and hooked me to tubes. Jeremiah's mouth had a big tube in it, but his panicked eyes told me, *Run away. Quick.* He was woozy.

He reached out a hand filled with needles and wires that made him look like a marionette. He scratched my chin because my ear had a needle in it.

I rolled onto my side and scooted so I could look him in the eye. Jeremiah tried to say something, but the tube stopped him. If I could have smiled, I would have. Neither of us could talk. Neither of us needed to.

Jeremiah looked up for a second, then back at me. Calm. He wasn't going to be afraid. He told me it was going to be okay. He had a tube in his mouth, but he still told me he loved me and that it would be all right. He told me not to be scared.

The only thing I'm afraid of is I won't get to see you again. I'm scared because I don't know what's going to happen to me, but I'm more scared it might not work, and I don't know what will happen to you. It bothers me that I won't ever find out if you made it. I love you, brother. I said. But Jeremiah only heard "Oink."

It was all he needed to hear.

CHAPTER FORTY-THREE

BOY

I woke up without my heart. Dr. Willis ripped it out and threw it in the trash.

I couldn't breathe on my own. I couldn't lick my dry lips. A plastic tube snaked into my mouth and toward my lungs. I wanted it out, but I needed it to breathe. It stopped me from talking or crying. It choked me but kept me alive.

At least everyone could see how much I was hurting, but they thought it was just because of the surgery. They didn't know that J6 filled my brain like that tube filled my throat. It hurt to think of him, but it hurt worse not to.

My family came in wearing gloves and masks. They

weren't allowed to touch me. That was fine. Dr. Willis was supposed to see us right away to tell us how the surgery had gone. She was five hours late. The nurses didn't know where she was and didn't see anything on her schedule, but when Dr. Willis finally made time for us, she told us about the "lab specimen" she had to operate on. Apparently, this "specimen" was more important than me. I thought about that pig in the recovery room and hoped he was okay. My family watched *Chopped* while we waited. After Dr. Willis left, my family was asked to leave.

One hour later, I cried when they ripped tape off my cheeks. Then they helped me cough the tube up. I gagged and choked until a foot of plastic came out of my mouth. I sucked in air like a new baby. A nurse used a toothbrush to rub moisturizer in my mouth and on my lips. For a second, I felt better. Then she stuck a breathing mask over my face. It was the kind they called an elephant trunk when I was little.

By nighttime, my head cleared up. I imagined J6's green pillow beside my bed. I knew that pillow was probably ruined in the flood, but if I went back it would still be there. Empty. Forever. My chest ached and the IVs itched. Being alive would hurt for a while. But the truth would hurt for the rest of my life.

I knew what they did to me. When Dr. Willis first explained it years ago, she told me not to research the operation. She said it would "freak me out." I went home and YouTubed a video that showed doctors cutting through a chest and opening the ribs like doors on a kitchen cabinet. They cut out my heart, got rid of it, and hooked up the new one. My body would hurt for a little while, but then I'd heal. I knew it would hurt more than I thought I could survive, but I'd still be okay. However, I also knew what happened to my brother. I knew they cut him open and took his heart. That hurt more than I could handle. I didn't think I'd ever fall asleep with these pictures in my head, but then I did.

The next day, someone decided I didn't need the elephant trunk. A physical therapist watched me eat ice chips. We moved on to water. I blew into a tube until the little yellow ball floated. I sat up in bed. I could almost make it to the gray plastic hospital potty with help. I pushed against her hand. She asked me to try to talk. I lay back down.

That night, the nurses asked me how I felt. I didn't answer them.

For a few hours the hospital went into lockdown. Gen-e-heart lost one of their hearts, and they needed to get it back. I knew how they felt.

In the ICU, visitors were only allowed in for two hours a day. Here they were "encouraged to stay as much as possible." They decided I shouldn't have any time alone. They conspired against my time to cry. Mom took nights, Dad took days. There was always someone in the room, but I still felt completely alone.

Jazmine would help out when she could, but she didn't try to get me to talk. She barely looked at me. Adnan's parents watched Justus.

Mom and Dad tried to trick me into talking about once an hour.

"Do you want to head home soon?"

"I'm sorry, I didn't hear what you said."

"Want to talk to your grandma on the phone? She's so worried."

I didn't have anything to say to them. The doctor thought something might be wrong. He thought I was "deprived of oxygen and incurred a brain injury." Dr. Willis said they just needed to give me time. I thought about talking, but then I remembered I wouldn't get to talk to my brother. I remembered whose fault that was. I couldn't stop seeing the empty pillow.

What if someone ate him? I wanted to throw up.

Every day Dr. Willis said the same thing. "Everything

is fine. Don't worry about Jeremiah Six. He's in a good place."

She said it like she desperately wanted me to believe it, but didn't actually want to explain what she was talking about. What good place? Wasn't he in the trash somewhere?

The remote was connected to the bed. I changed the channel. I'd had enough Food Network.

When Mom came back from the bathroom and saw that I was watching an R-rated movie on TV, she knew my brain wasn't hurt. She changed it to some home-renovation show.

"How are you doing?" asked Mom.

I didn't answer.

"I understand how you feel, honey," she lied.

No one could know how I felt because no one else knew him like I did. He was barely six months old. He never even got to smash his own birthday cake. After Mom fell asleep while sitting in the corner chair, I cried and shook and everything hurt.

One morning, Dad brought Justus.

He whispered to her, "Jerry isn't talking a lot, but that's okay. He's just really tired and confused."

I shot him a look. Justus caught it. She smiled.

"Daddy, can you let me talk to him by myself for a minute?"

"I'll be down the hall." He stepped outside, but he didn't pull the door closed. Justus didn't know he was eavesdropping. I didn't care.

"Jerry?" she whispered, searching my face. I cleared my throat.

I watched the movie that wouldn't stop playing in my brain. I pictured that empty pillow.

"Jerry?" That voice sounded the way I felt. Justus's face drove those pictures away. She started to cry. My arms were too tangled in IVs and wires to let her on the bed, but I wanted to hug her.

"Where is J6? What happened? No one will tell me."

Justus had two brothers. Now she had one. "J6 won't come back home," I said.

"Where is he?"

I looked at her and my mind calmed back down.

"He's dead."

"How do you know?"

I pointed at my chest. "He's a part of me now. That means you need to play with me like you played with him. You need to teach me the way you taught him. Because he's not all the way dead. Does that make sense?"

"No."

I took a breath. "I miss him so much. I am going to need you to hang out with me."

She nodded. "That makes sense."

I wondered if she was even more upset about this than I was. We both knew she played with him more than I did. She talked to him longer. She was there for him before I got over myself enough to pay attention, and yet she was here offering to make me feel better.

Dad smiled when he came back in. I smiled back.

That night Jazmine showed up with Mom.

"Can I talk to my sister?" I asked.

"Um, sure," said Mom. She grinned and wanted to stay, too. Instead, she dropped her bag and let the door shut behind her and Dad.

The room was quiet until Jazmine put her hand on the side of my bed. She was the only one who still wore a mask in to see me.

"He wanted to save you," she said.

"They killed him."

"You're not honoring his memory. He wanted to save you, and he gave up his heart for you. He gave you a gift, and you need to accept it."

It sounded like she thought I was trying to hog the ball again and not take his help.

Jazmine hugged at my head. Her arms were stiff. She used to hug me all the time when I was young and cute. Then, a few years ago, I thought it was funny to duck out of her arms. We were out of practice now and my chest was off limits, so the weird head squeeze was the best we could do.

She took her phone out of her pocket and handed it to me. She was on Instagram. J6 was everywhere, and he would be forever. I stared at him, and I couldn't see that pillow anymore. I shut my eyes for a second to see if I could still find him inside. I saw him dancing at the farm because he couldn't resist being the center of attention. I smiled.

"I'll bring your tablet tomorrow," she said. "Borrow my phone for tonight. Don't go through my texts. Don't get into my WhatsApp. Don't post anything. And don't use all my data."

"Um." I looked at her phone. Then I looked up at her.

"And don't hate Mom and Dad. They didn't know he was smart. Hate me."

I squeezed her hand. I'd do better by my sister. I'd bake her next birthday cake. I'd be as good a brother to her as J6 was to me. But then I thought about everything she did. I didn't have it in my heart to forgive her, but that didn't matter. My heart was gone. My sisters saved my life. My mom, my dad, and Dr. Willis all saved my life. My brother's heart couldn't hate any of them, and I had his heart. And I had my sisters' hearts. And my parents' hearts. I had them this whole time.

But they didn't really have mine until now.

J6's heart came with forgiveness.

I took a deep breath in. I was breathing because of him. And it hurt. That breath pulled at my stiches and made my broken ribs ache. Everything hurt. For now. But not forever. And it was all because of J6.

Jazmine smiled and turned to the EKG. She cocked her head to the side and said, "Listen."

I closed my eyes.

Beep, beep, beep, sang the EKG beside me.

Jazmine was barely paying attention to me. "It's like I can hear him," she said.

And then I heard him, too. I felt him. I always would.

CHAPTER FORTY-FOUR

PIG

Everything was dark and it felt like my head was packed with pillow guts. My mouth was propped wide open. They did it.

They finally stuck an apple in there.

I slowly tried opening my eyes, but they were crusty like I'd been sleeping for a long time. I was somewhere bright with humming sounds and footsteps. Maybe it was hog heaven and I'd see my brothers. I tried to oink, but I couldn't.

A person without a face appeared in my blurry world.

I blinked, and when I opened my eyes, Dr. Willis was staring at me.

I didn't have an apple in my mouth. It was just a tube. If it was an apple, I'd at least have a snack.

"Can you understand me?"

I couldn't nod my head or oink, so I didn't know what she was expecting. I tried to give her a look that told her how ridiculous she sounded.

"Can you move your legs?"

I tried to kick her so she'd get this tube out of my throat. It didn't work.

"Jeremiah's okay. I know that you chose to save him, so I saved you."

Wait, what?

"But I'll get in trouble for stealing the heart I used on you, so I have to go. Don't worry. You'll be okay."

She left me there lying on an icy table without even a blue blanket to keep me warm. It was the least snuggly place I'd ever been, but I couldn't keep my eyes open.

"Hurry!"

A voice ripped me out of a wonderful dream. I was the king of a place called Pizzatown, and my throne was made out of burritos. I didn't want to open my eyes and lose my kingdom. Dr. Willis would just ask me silly questions. Plus, my chest hurt a lot. Even worse than that time the avocado tried to murder me.

I was just about to get back to dreamland when the voice spoke again.

"Let's make sure to get them all. She said there should be about nineteen. Check room twenty-three."

It wasn't Dr. Willis. It was a beautiful voice. What was going on? I moved my mouth. The tube was gone.

I opened my eyes, and all I saw was a bright light. Then a magical figure appeared in front of me. I blinked and noticed a smile, a tattoo, and a buzzcut.

An angel.

FOUR
MONTHS
LATER

CHAPTER FORTY-FIVE

BOY

Jazmine pulled up to the Rescue Ranch's visitor's center. Everything on the way in seemed like it felt just like I did: exhausted.

Looking through the pollen-covered window, I could barely see the volunteers in their yellow shirts scurrying around with some little vested animal, but they looked busy. Even the cows seemed like they were ready for a nap. I was awake for most of last night, and it wasn't because I slept in the living room of our new apartment. It was because that tiny space stuffed with five people still felt lonely.

My finger poked the scar on my chest. Anyone could see the line slicing the length of my rib cage, but it just looked like a cut on the skin. Really, the incision went more than halfway to my back, but the scars felt deeper. I knew they took my bad heart out, but I'm not sure they put anything in its place. I had to accept that this hollowed-out feeling was just normal now. Jokes would be a little less funny and good news would be less exciting. Dad said that it'd get better, but that didn't seem likely.

Everything would just be "less."

A few weeks ago, Emily called Jazmine to invite us over to the Rescue Ranch. I guess that's one way to get people to volunteer. At first I didn't really want to go, but Jazmine finally convinced me. Justus was excited. As soon as the van stopped, she rushed out.

"I guess we need to go inside," I said, but I didn't move.

I didn't want to face Emily yet. The only time I'd met her was the worst day of my life.

"We're a little early. No one will care if we take a lap around," Jazmine said. I felt relieved.

In the distance there was a red barn that might have jumped right out of a painting. I headed in that direction. I thought Jazmine might wait by the car, or Justus would be in some animal's pen by now, but they stayed by my side. I wasn't alone.

This place felt calm. These animals probably thought

they were out of hope, and then they arrived here. We found a little stream and followed it toward the pens.

"There they are!" Justus shouted. She sprinted toward the pigpen.

"Go on," Jazmine said to me. "She wants you to go with her."

Justus was leaning over the fence and flopping her arms around so hard, she looked like an inflatable tube guy beside a car dealership.

"Not yet," I said.

I wasn't sure I could face them. Hearing their oinks hurt. Jazmine gave me a side hug.

I didn't really have sisters until I got my brother, but I knew I could get through this with them by my side.

Justus ran back to us and grabbed both of our hands.

"Hurry up!"

She pulled so hard that she would have fallen if we'd let her go.

"We're coming!" I said. There was nothing in that pen that could be this important.

Seeing the pigs brought back memories, just like I thought they would. The first one I saw was sticking his head through the fence and wagging his tail. His spots looked like J6, but he was dirty. A lot of the pigs had spots and it creeped me out. Like seeing a ghost.

"Jerry, look! That one!

"Justus, I see him. I get it. I know who he looks like."

"No. You don't get it. It *is* him," she said.

I let myself hope that somehow, he got saved. Somehow, he ended up here. Somehow, somehow, somehow. I hoped for a hundred impossible things as I leaned over the fence and studied the pig while he studied me with a happy, curious face. He seemed like a great pig. But he wasn't my brother.

"Justus, it's not him. His ear, no tattoo."

I said it quietly. Almost a whisper. I didn't really want her to hear. I wanted her to believe for a few more seconds. But I didn't need the tattoo to know it wasn't J6. I could tell by the way this pig looked at me.

"Oh," Justus said, deflated. It was as if we had unplugged one of those tube guys from a car dealership.

"But I think he likes you, Justus."

He did. Everyone liked Justus. She nodded but looked disappointed.

"J6 would never live in a pigsty anyway," Jazmine said. "That's why he liked my room more than Jeremiah's."

Justus smiled.

"We should find Emily," I said. Seeing her couldn't be worse than the fake J6.

We didn't talk on our way back. I felt ridiculous. For

a second, I thought he was here. I thought it was possible, but it wasn't. If I could deal with that without breaking down, then I was ready to volunteer.

The three of us stopped on the porch. It was so hopeful outside, and for the first time I could see my way to getting better.

I walked up to the door and reached for the knob.

But a squeal in the distance stopped me.

I turned around, and a loose pig was barreling across the ranch. He could run into traffic. I guess I'd have to start my volunteering sooner than I thought. I walked toward him. It shouldn't be hard to catch him since he was heading straight for us.

"Oink."

That oink sounded so familiar. Maybe a lot of pigs sounded like J6?

The pig was wearing a service-animal-type vest that was the same yellow as the T-shirts the volunteers wore. It even said RESCUE RANCH VOLUNTEER on it, just like the shirts. And under that, in smaller letters, it said, PET ME.

My smile knew before I did. I let loose a little shout, and I took off running faster than my new doctor recommended. The muscles in my legs came back to life, just like the rest of me.

Just like him.

We crashed into each other laughing and oinking. Justus was right behind and about to tackle him when she stopped. She pointed at his chest. His scar matched mine exactly.

We hugged him for what felt like forever. Even Jazmine patted his head. Then I felt sadness creeping in where it didn't belong. I sat up a little and looked around me. He was happy here. I'd been having a really tough time, and he was here all along. Living his best life. Without me.

"I guess you didn't need me after all. You have it made," I said.

He hit me with his head, gave me a look, and said, "Oink."

Justus rolled her eyes. "No, Jerry. He was waiting for us."

He nodded. "Oink?"

This one meant "What took you so long?"

I looked him in the eyes and felt his heart under my hand.

"Thank you."

"Oink."

And he didn't need to spell anything out for me. This time I knew what it meant. *Oink* meant everything.

AUTHOR'S NOTE

In January 2017, scientists injected human cells into piglets that hadn't been born yet. The new growing creatures weren't pigs anymore. They were a mixture of animals called chimeras. I started writing *Pighearted* the week after that experiment was announced because I couldn't get a question out of my head: How hard should you fight to save someone's life?

The summer after my freshman year of college, my boyfriend's (now husband's) mom had a heart attack. We tried to take care of her, but what she really needed was a heart transplant. She was one of eighteen million people killed that year by heart disease. Medical devices like ICDs keep hearts beating and LVADs pump blood, but many patients will still run out of time waiting for a new heart.

Some researchers are so desperate to find a way to help that they want to use gene-editing technology and human stem cells to create chimeras that grow human organs. They imagine huge pig farms that produce organs instead of bacon, but there's a problem. The pigs aren't pigs. They're part human, and even scientists doing the experiments are afraid that the stem cells they inject could make their way into the brain. That would mean that these creatures might be able to have human thoughts and feelings like J6. That makes this research extremely controversial. And its funding is restricted and could be outlawed any day.

It'd be wrong to let a person die or to kill a chimera. It seemed like a lose-lose situation until I learned about how scientists are growing organs in jars instead of animals. They start with a heart that is unsuitable for transplant. They strip away the cells and leave only connective tissue. Then they use skin cells to create new heart cells that cover the skeleton-like structure, and finally they let it grow. Unfortunately, it will take years to get from a heart in a jar to a practical treatment that could save lives, but in *Pighearted* I imagine that it could happen tomorrow.

Today, Jeremiah's heart condition, hypertrophic cardiomyopathy, affects one out of every five hundred people. Like those thousands of other kids, Jeremiah isn't defined by his medical experiences, and his struggles go beyond his heart condition. I've tried to imagine what

Jeremiah and J6 would go through after consulting with cardiologists and LVAD patients, but I still don't know how far we should go to save someone's life.

There are many questions I can't answer, and neither can *Pighearted*, but I hope Jeremiah and J6 are a reminder that we should never stop fighting for the ones we love.

For more information, check out some of these resources:

Gabrielle-Ann A. Torre, et al. "Mending a Broken Heart—The Genetics of Heart Disease." Frontiers for Young Minds, kids.frontiersin.org/article/10.3389/frym.2018.00019.

Hesmen Saey, Tina. "2020 chemistry Nobel goes for CRISPR, the gene-editing tool." *Science News for Students*, 16 Nov. 2020, sciencenewsforstudents.org/article/2020-chemistry-nobel-gene-editing-tool-crispr.

Ossola, Alexandra. "Scientists Grow Full-Sized, Beating Human Hearts From Stem Cells." *Popular Science*, March 16, 2016, popsci.com/scientists-grow-transplantable-hearts-with-stem-cells/.

Stein, Rob. "In Search For Cures, Scientists Create Embryos That Are Both Animal And Human." *All Things Considered*, NPR, May 18, 2016, npr .org/sections/health-shots/2016/05/18/478212837 /in-search-for-cures-scientists-create-embryos-that -are-both-animal-and-human.

ACKNOWLEDGMENTS

So many people helped this book come to be. I consider them pighearted. Thanks to:

Melissa Nasson, my agent, for believing in my pig tale and finding it the right home. There's no one I'd rather have fighting for this story.

Samantha Gentry, my editor, who saw exactly how to make this pig fly off the page. Thank you to the team at Little, Brown Books for Young Readers: Megan Tingley, Jackie Engel, Alvina Ling, David Caplan, Sasha Illingworth, Karina Granda, Jenny Kimura, Marisa Finklestein, Thandile Jackson, Stefanie Hoffman, Shanese Mullins, Mara Brashem, and Victoria Stapleton. And to Ramona Kaulitzki, who brought Jeremiah and J6 to life on a cover that went far beyond what I could have hoped for.

Dana Mele, whose mentorship in Author Mentor Match was brilliant and exactly what I needed. Rebecca Petruck, whose insight transformed *Pighearted*.

The River Valley Writers who listened to me read

the novel aloud four pages at a time: R. Lee Fryar, Jennette Gahlot, Cathy Graves, and Marianne Horton. The Houston Writer's Guild, who knew just what I needed to fix: Lauran Kerr-Heraly, Race Blazek, Pat Daily, and Joan Jyakhwa, Brenda Preuss, and Ollie Stevenson.

All the subject matter experts who helped bring this book to life. I knew Dr. Frederick White would help me with the cardiological details of the story, but he also helped me through the medical-ethical labyrinth. Thanks to the other experts, my cousins Claire, Haley, Logan, Cassie, Savanna, and Jackson, who set me straight on everything from the details of soccer to whether kids these days say "left on read" (they do).

Teachers everywhere, but especially Becca Blank, who read and critiqued a very early, very bad version of this story, and to Morgan Lambertson, Elston Craver, and all the amazing kids we taught at YES Prep Fifth Ward.

My dad, Tony Perry, who taught me to read, and then to write, and then made me believe that I could make it. My sister, Taylor Perry, who proofread and inspired me with her creativity, work ethic, and daring.

My husband, Robert, and our daughter, Ada, who made it possible for me to write by having much more faith in me than I have in myself.

And thank you, Mom. I miss you.

Alex Perry used to teach middle schoolers in Houston, but now she writes books for kids everywhere. When she was six, she babysat a potbellied piglet, and she's been obsessed with his cuteness ever since. She just had to get that messy little guy into a book, and now she has. She lives in Arkansas with a messy little human baby, her husband, and two huge dogs. *Pighearted* is her debut novel. She invites you to visit her at alexperrybooks.com or follow her on Twitter @Alextheadequate.